KIDNAPPED

A CRIME OF PASSION

I0619510

J. Brinkley

Table of Contents

CHAPTER ONE

The office that Blair worked in always felt so cold, like there was a constant cool draft wisping its way through the cubicles that were spread out in the space. For a while, she thought that they just kept the place cold all of the time for some reason, perhaps to salvage the high-tech computers that she and the rest of her co-workers used to do their job. Lately, she'd began to believe that it felt cold because she constantly got chills from the nature of the work that she had to do.

Blair became a specialized government agent a few years ago. She handled high-security clearance information across multiple sectors of the government, making sure the right information went to the right people and that it was all stored correctly and securely. She saw behind the curtain, becoming exposed to the harsh truths of reality, of society. There was so much that ordinary citizens didn't know about their country. Of course, there were conspiracies and jokes, but people really had no idea what was going on around them.

Even in the small things that they thought the government had no interest or business in, they were there, manipulating the system to their own gain. Secrets flowed like blood, and there was no patching up that wound. She just worked to direct the flow, to conceal it behind metaphorical bandages from the public eye. Whether it was the Department of Education or the Food and Drug Administration, things were never as they seemed, and there was always a reason behind every little decision.

All of the secrets that she uncovered, ranging from population control tactics to undisclosed carcinogens in foods that no one expected, filled her with anxiety and nausea. It was awful what the government was doing to their own people. They were manipulating them, slowly killing them, controlling them. She wanted to cry wolf, to wave a red flag, to let everyone know what was really happening in their society, but she couldn't. Upon taking the job, she signed extensive contracts and nondisclosure agreements. If she breathed a single secret, she would be jailed forever, fined until she didn't have a single thing to her name. She would essentially be wiped off of the face of the Earth.

Blair nervously bit at her thumb nail as she sent a few encrypted, secure files to a receiver in the Bureau of Alcohol, Tobacco, Firearms and Explosives. She'd only glanced through the files to make sure that all of the necessary information was there, unable to properly stomach reading through the weapons of destruction that were being crafted. She couldn't even imagine the death toll, and she really didn't want to.

Blair had always been a nervous soul, unable to start a fight or confront people. It just wasn't in her nature. Bouncing from foster home to foster home hadn't made her all that great in a social sense, and there were too many complicated feelings for her to try to properly express. It made her a quiet person naturally, but she didn't want to be quiet about things like this. She wanted to help people, to inform the public of the despicable nature of the government, but how could her soft-spoken self even begin to do that?

She never wanted to be involved in any of this. She was in her late twenties, shifting toward the middle point of her life. After getting out of foster care, she worked front-desk jobs to normal office desk jobs, learning the skills of information handling. She never went to college, knowing that she needed to focus on getting money to just live first. She lived in an apartment that was roach-infested with things always breaking. She lost her last office job because of cutbacks. She was desperate to get anything at all.

At the time, she thought she'd struck gold because a recruiter reached out to her, aligning her with the job that she had now. She passed the interviews with a resume tailored to information handling and security and landed the job. It gave her great pay and great benefits. It was more money than she'd ever seen before in her life. How could she turn it down? At the time, she hadn't really known what kind of information that she would be handling. They only told her it'd be important government documents.

She couldn't believe what those important government documents contained. At first, they gave her light things to process and handle. They weren't really deep secrets. They were just fact files, descriptions, profiles, and things like that. As she did her job and gained their trust, they gave her the heavier things. At this point, years later, Blair was in this so deep. She didn't even know her way out of this place now. She needed the money, which helped her get a better apartment and a better car. She needed the benefits, which allowed her to go to the doctor without worrying about too high of a bill. She needed those things, but she felt like she was playing a villain.

She was helping deceive millions of innocent people, and she couldn't do anything to help them unless she wanted to risk her own life. She finally felt like she was just being able to live. After struggling with her parents dying one after the other when she was younger, being thrown into the foster care system, being unable to develop deep relationships with other people, this job seemed like her big break. She could buy the things that she needed and wanted. She could actually breathe for once. She even took a vacation. Those seemed like small things to some, but they were huge to her because she'd never been able to experience them until now.

Blair felt stuck, and it wasn't like she could talk to anyone about this. If she opened her mouth, her life was as good as over. She drifted a hand up through her dark hair, its waves falling along the black blazer that she wore over a white blouse and paired with a black pencil skirt and heels. She knew that she needed to relax, especially since the small, dim office she worked in was always watched. Her brown eyes shifted to the security camera in the front right corner of the room, which had a perfect view of her desk. There were two rows of cubicles in the room, and she was right in the middle of the left row. At least she was closest to the door.

Once she sent the files over, she sat back in her chair, taking some time before moving on to the next task. Her productivity had been going down a bit lately. It was discouraging doing this kind of work, and she figured that if she slowed down her pace, maybe all of the wrongdoings would slow down a little too. She felt that was the only thing that she could contribute to the rest of the world. Other than that, she felt useless. She *always* felt useless.

She had no partner to help support or care for. She hardly had any friends to do favors for or listen to. She had no family to visit. It was just her, and she wanted to help someone. She wanted a purpose in life, to have goals and plans for herself. She felt like she lived day to day, just getting on by, not thinking for herself or for her future. It was like she was just existing, and she was tired of living like that. She wanted to be a force for change, but she had no idea how to be that.

Luckily, Blair didn't have to do any more incriminating work for at least another hour. It was time for her lunch break, which meant quietly picking at a sandwich that she packed in the back corner of the break room at one of the wooden tables in there. Her five other co-workers ate in there as well, but she didn't really talk to them all that much. They were also a bit quiet, nearly secretive, but she didn't invade their business. She felt too invasive at this point, knowing more than she should.

With a deep breath, Blair stood from her chair before pushing it back under her desk. She headed out of the main office before her co-workers and walked down the hall to the first door on the right, where the break room was located. Before she walked in, her eyes shifted down the hall to the end, where a tall, fair-skinned security guard was posted. He was always there, but she didn't know his name or anything. Shrugging to herself, she made a beeline to the fridge, pulling out her chicken salad sandwich in a Ziploc bag before taking her usual seat in the back corner. The chair was wooden and uncomfortable, but she rested back in it regardless. It was better than being back in her cubicle doing awful, dirty work.

Blair pulled her sandwich out of her bag and took one bite, feeling like she was chewing on cardboard. When she was at work, she usually lost her appetite, and that didn't change today. It was hard to stomach anything around here. She fell back into the brief silence of the room before her co-workers came in, her eyes closing briefly for a moment. She willed herself to be anywhere but there.

However, she had five hours left of work, and she knew that they would tick by ridiculously slow. She just had to hold out for those five hours, go home to recharge and cope, and then repeat the cycle the next day and the next day. One day, she would break out of this cycle. She would become someone that she could be proud of, but that day just wasn't today. She just hoped she wouldn't have to keep on telling herself that until her last day. If she wanted to make a difference, she had to take a chance, and that meant facing her fears. The world all around her was scary, and she was right in the middle of it all. She would fight her way out. Someday.

CHAPTER TWO

Blair peered up from eating her chicken salad sandwich as the rest of her co-workers filed into the break room. It was like they were split into two groups. The supervisor of the group, Quentin, along with two other workers, Melody and Dominic, always seemed to gravitate toward each other, sitting together at the table next to hers. The other two workers, Wanda and Terry, sat at the other table closer to the door, but they didn't seem to be friends. They just didn't sit with her or Quentin's group.

"Hey, Thompson." Quentin's voice broke through Blair's mental lull as he moved to stand in front of her table.

Blair tilted her head up at Quentin, her eyes starting to match the wideness of an owl's as she looked up at him. She hardly talked to Quentin, and it wasn't because he was particularly scary or anything. He was probably in his late thirties with a muscular build and trimmed brown hair. His skin was a smooth, tan color, and he always wore blue or white button-downs with black slacks. He just looked like a normal guy, but the whole thing with him being her supervisor worried her a bit. If someone was going to get onto her for not doing her job right, it would be him, and she couldn't risk getting fired or sent to jail for any reason.

"Yes?" she asked him, feeling her heart hammer against her chest. She wondered if he was about to scold her for something. She hadn't been as productive as usual, adopting a slower pace, but she'd still done her work on time.

"I just wanted to ask how you were doing," Quentin replied, his head tilting a little as the side of his mouth quirked up in a faint smile.

Blair didn't know how to respond to that. She'd been expecting him to say something different. Her eyes shifted to the side, just past him, to look at Melody and Dominic, who were trying to discreetly look her way. They were closer to her in age, probably around their early thirties. Melody wore her long, black hair up in a ponytail, contrasting against the soft, olive tone of her skin. Dominic looked like he was right out of college with a clean-shaven baby face, a shaved head, light-brown skin, and hazel eyes that seemed to glow. They didn't seem like the type to work here, but she didn't feel like the type to work here either. She didn't know the circumstances that brought them here.

"Fine. I'm fine," Blair replied, nearly stumbling over her words as she turned back to Quentin.

"Good. I just noticed you've kind of been lagging behind the others pace-wise," Quentin commented, his voice coming out soft, but he sounded starkly curious.

Blair felt a flush of panic rush through her at his words, realizing that they *had* noticed her slack in productivity. She'd only slowed down a little bit. It wasn't like she was ignoring assignments or waiting until the last minute to finish them.

"Oh, I'm sorry about that. I've… just been under the weather a bit lately. Headache and such," Blair replied, scrambling for any excuse that she could possibly find. She didn't need them to be suspicious of her loyalty to her department, to the government, despite her losing any respect or trust that she had in them. If she were rich and stable, she would ditch this job in a heartbeat, but that wasn't her reality. Everything she needed rested on her having this job.

Quentin took a moment before humming and nodding, his smile broadening just a little. "I hope you feel better soon," he merely replied before turning and heading back to the table that Melody and Dominic were seated at.

Blair stared after him, wondering if it were safe for her to even move at this point. She felt like her every move was watched, and that was most likely the case. She needed to be more careful, but it was hard to behave perfectly when her job pretty much disgusted her.

She eventually turned back to her sandwich, feeling like she was staring at a slab of concrete. She'd officially lost the remainder of her appetite, prompting her to toss the rest of her lunch away and then head back to her desk to waste the rest of her break until it was over.

Quietly, she chewed on her bottom lip, her eyes shifting to the security camera in the corner. How closely were they watching her? Deep within her chest, she felt something stir, something like a darkness that hid in the deepest parts of her. After years and years of dealing with neglect, instability, and abuse during her time in the foster care system, she experienced a lot of negativity mentally, and she never found a good way to cope with that. She had no one to talk to. She couldn't afford a therapist. She just bottled it up, shoving it down deep. In some instances of extreme stress, it tried to make its appearance again, to play a part in her life, but she tried to shove it back down as much as she possibly could.

Blair didn't want to be an angry person. She wanted to be calm and collected, but it was so hard to keep that side of her at bay with everything going on at work. How the government deceived people and tried to ruin them on purpose made her nearly boil over, and, as someone who dealt with injustice throughout adolescence, she hated just standing by and letting that happen to other innocent people that didn't deserve it at all.

In some instances, Blair wished that she could turn a blind eye to everything, to just look the other way and keep her mouth shut. Her life would be so much easier if she could just do that and behave like she was expected to. However, her conscience just didn't want to allow her to do that. It made her want to scream every single incriminating secret from the rooftop of this place, to open up everyone's eyes.

Blair didn't even know that she was glaring at the security camera until her co-workers started to file inside the office, coaxing her to quickly look down. She shook her head at herself, willing herself to collect herself. She'd already slipped up evidently, so she needed to keep her head down and work. Her eyes shifted up a little, meeting Quentin's gaze as he walked inside, heading his desk in the front left row. She wondered if there was another reason why he was watching her so closely. It wasn't like she could ask him without making him more curious than he already seemed. The safest thing for her to do was ignore him and just hope deeply that he ignored her right back. Ignorance was safety here, and she needed to act like the most ignorant person in this entire government building in the depths of New York City.

CHAPTER THREE

Things started to take an odd turn at work for Blair. She noticed that things felt different. Strange. She felt like she constantly had to pitch a look over her shoulder, like someone was trailing her, but it was always just her own shadow. No one was ever there. She thought she was going crazy, creating odd scenarios in her head that were probably just due to stress. She really needed to relax, but it was hard to when her employer was the government, who actively went against its own citizens. Just because she was an employee didn't mean that she was exempt from their corruption.

What really confirmed to her that things were strange was when her boss walked into the office. Quentin was a supervisor for her small department, but he wasn't the head boss. He was just the link between the workers and the head of the department. Simon Polk was the head of the information handling department, and he was the scary one that lurked around. He was an older man, in his fifties, with thin, white hair, light stubble, icy-blue eyes, and stark, pale skin. He always wore full black suits, and he reminded Blair of a reaper. He was one not to cross.

Blair hadn't had many interactions with Simon, but stories regarding him floated through the department enough for her to get a feel of how he was as a boss and as a person. He was harsh and sharp, not taking any lip from anyone. He wanted things to be perfect. He wanted his workers to be obedient. She wondered why he decided to pay a random visit to the department, which was an incredibly rare thing for him to do. He was usually coming up with evil master plans with the rest of the heads of other government departments. To what did her department owe the pleasure this time?

"Tuck your shirt in, boy! What are you thinking?" Simon immediately snapped at Dominic, who just stared up at him with a look of disbelief for a second before hurriedly tucking his button-down into his slacks.

Melody immediately ducked her head, making sure her blouse was smoothed down, while Quentin sat up straight as a board at his desk.

Blair wished she could sink through the floor right now, especially since Simon was making his way down the aisle closer to her. She felt she looked fine dress-wise, but she could already hear a lecture about her work ethic, despite her working as hard as she could for the past few days. She didn't want to be on the radar, and she thought that she entered the clear, but seeing Simon here in person told her otherwise.

Simon eyed Blair for a few seconds as he walked closer, but he ended up walking right past her much to her surprise.

Blair believed that she was just hearing things, but she could've sworn that she heard a really low and faint chuckle sound from Simon as he walked past her. What could possibly be funny? Did she have something on her face that she didn't know about? Her hand quickly darted around her face, feeling for anything that seemed humorous, but she couldn't find anything. That just made her more nervous because now she really had no idea why he was laughing under his breath.

"Your top responsibility is privacy. You are the gatekeepers of our nation's most vital information. You swore to provide security and safety to this confidential information. If you violate this, you will face consequences," Simon lectured as he turned and walked back up the aisle toward the front of the room. He crossed his arms over his broad chest, his eyes gliding over everyone, like he was surveying his own kingdom.

"Exercise discretion at all times," Simon emphasized, his eyes moving to Blair's briefly before he nodded to Quentin. With a soft huff, he spun on his heel and nearly marched out of the office, leaving Blair overcome with nervous chills.

Was that last part directed at her? She could hardly be sure since he was addressing the entire department. She wondered what coaxed him to say such a thing at this certain time. Were they suspicious of someone? Was it her? Besides slowing down her work, she hadn't done anything that could risk getting her in trouble. She was completely secretive when it came to her job. In fact, if someone in public asked about her job, she just said that she was a desk worker. She gave no one any indication that she was working for the government because she didn't want to be put in a situation where people threatened her for secrets.

"You heard him, guys," Quentin announced to the department as he turned in his chair toward the back. He glanced at the door to make sure that Simon was really gone before glancing in the direction of Melody and Dominic. "Discretion or oppression," he whispered, a smirk crossing his lips as the others laughed beneath their breaths.

A confused look crossed Blair's face at their behavior, but they did seem to be friends. They must've just been joking around to lighten the mood because Simon was pretty daunting to anyone. It was just strange for Quentin, who was a supervisor that seemed pretty serious about his job, to say something like that. This wasn't a department that really joked about things.

Pushing past those conflicting thoughts, Blair pulled up her email to check her assignments for today. She worked through assignment after assignment, organizing information and getting it to the right people. She only took a break for lunch before getting right back at it, trying to get done so that she could go home. She only had fifteen minutes of work left when she suddenly got an email directly from Simon. That never happened before.

Blair opened the email, a confused look gracing her face as she read through the text. He'd sent her an urgent assignment to do before she went home today, which was a rare thing to happen. She worked a little overtime before, but this would take her at least an hour to wrap up and finish. Why did he have to send it to her out of all the other workers in the office? She looked up to watch the others start to leave the office, essentially abandoning her in the dim space. She worked as quickly as she could, wanting to get home before it got dark, but she had a feeling that wouldn't be the case.

The assignment's content didn't even seem that urgent. It was just about pulling money from the Environmental Protection Agency and lining the pockets of the congressmen more. It was despicable, but she just really wanted to go home, so she organized the information and prepared to get it sent off to the right people. She could complain about how unfair the situation was later in the comfort and safety of her bed in her apartment. Home was the only place where she felt safe lately.

"Night, Blair." Quentin's voice suddenly broke through her thoughts.

Blair looked up with a confused expression, not expecting Quentin to still be in the office with her. She could've sworn that she saw him leave with Melody and Dominic like he usually did. They'd been close ever since she had been hired, and it seemed like they'd gotten even closer over the years.

"Good night," she murmured, sounding more like a question than a reply.

He spoke to her on occasion, and it was usually just him being polite and greeting her. However, he'd been acknowledging her a bit more than usual lately. Yesterday, he made a comment about how her work was getting done faster. The day before, he nearly tried to chat with her about one of the assignments that she was working on. It might seem normal in the grand scheme of socialization, but Blair just wasn't used to that sort of interaction from Quentin. It wasn't like they were friends.

"I'll keep an eye out for you in the morning," Quentin told her, giving her a faint smile before nodding and stepping out of the office, leaving Blair alone with her confusion.

Blair wasn't sure what he meant by that. Maybe he meant that he would keep an eye out for her to greet her or something. It wasn't like he was a mean person, but things just felt weird lately. She just had to take Quentin's sudden interest in her into account amongst all of the other things that had been happening lately.

She considered searching for a new job, but she didn't want to start all over again. Getting an interview was hard and took forever, especially if there were multiple rounds of them. She just couldn't risk the gap in pay right now. She just had to hold tight, get this work done, and keep quiet. That was all that was required of her. When she got in a better place, she could think about how to leverage the power and knowledge that she had, which was more than the average citizen.

CHAPTER FOUR

B y the time that Blair finally wrapped up all of her work and sent out the information, the entire building was empty, and it was pitch-black outside. She grabbed her things from her cubicle, which was completely bare compared to the spaces belonging to her co-workers. They had pictures of their families and little figurines. She had no pictures to hang up, so she left it bare besides a few pens and sticky notes. It would suffice. She wasn't trying to get comfy in this place anyway.

Once she stood from her desk, she made her way down the aisle, her hand reaching up to switch off the dim LED light illuminating the space. She didn't want to come back tomorrow, but she didn't have a choice in the matter. As a child, she thought being an adult meant she could make any and all decisions, like she was the ruler of her own life. Reality had been harsh to her once she grew up. She soon learned she hardly had any independence or freedom as an adult. She played by the government's rules, which told her to work a job until she died, or she would die sooner, whether that was from lack of shelter, food, water, or medical care. It was an awful game to play.

Blair walked out of the office and down the hallway toward the door that would lead out to the level in the parking garage that she'd parked her car on. It wasn't a fancy car. It was used and had a decent amount of miles already on it, but it hadn't broken down on her yet. That was what counted. Before, she was catching city buses or just walking everywhere. Being in her car with the heat turned up during the middle of winter was a blessing, and it beat trudging through the snow wrapped in a million layers. She still ended up getting sick. That meant dollar store chicken noodle soup or a shot of whiskey as her substitute for healthcare. Now, she could just go to the doctor or go get medicine. Some things just amounted to the whole world for her.

A soft thud suddenly sounded behind her, prompting her to spin around. All she saw was the darkness of the hallway. An eerie feeling crept up the length of her spine as she stared blankly ahead. She could be staring at something in the dark, and she'd have no idea because she couldn't see anything. The thought alone nearly made her sick, so she just turned back around, giving up on trying to see what that noise happened to be. It could've just been the fridge in the break room making noise. It could be the building just settling. She gave herself every logical explanation that she could as she headed down the rest of the hallway toward the door. Even a ghost sounded more comforting than some of the things that she considered.

It was so late that even the security guard usually at the door wasn't there anymore. Once her hand grabbed the doorknob of the heavy door, she twisted and pushed, soft light gracing her from the parking garage. It was dimly lit out there, but she could at least make out what was in front of her. She walked under the flickering lights, grabbing her purse and phone tightly in her hands as she walked through the nearly empty parking garage floor. Of course, she was parked way in the back near the ramp heading to the level below her own. The clacking of her heels on concrete echoed throughout the floor. She was up on the third level, which was mainly the information handling department's floor. Other departments were on other floors doing their own corrupt thing.

Luckily for Blair, it was fall. She didn't have to worry about freezing out here as she headed across the parking garage. However, she still felt a chill down her neck. Her breaths started to come out shakily, anxiety gripping her as the space between her and her car seemed to not get any closer. It was like she was walking on a treadmill.

Her eyes shifted around, brushing over the few cars in the parking garage. She knew that some people left their cars here overnight and got rides from other people. It was still eerie to see them just sitting there, though.

Blair gasped as the bottom of her heel clipped the concrete, making her trip and hit the ground on her knees and palms. She winced as the concrete grated against her palms, scraping them up to expose red. She dusted her hands, trying to coax away the sting as she crouched there on her knees, which were also marked up. She couldn't believe how clumsy she was being. She needed to breathe and calm down before she somehow knocked herself out just trying to get to her car.

With a deep breath, she glanced over her shoulder, turning her head every which way to search the area. She was completely alone. All she could hear was the sounds of the city outside of the parking garage with its honking, shouting, and cars heading down the street. She told herself that everything was normal. She made the walk a million times to her car from work before. The only difference this time was it was dark, and the parking garage was just a little emptier. That was it. Everything else was in her mind.

Her greatest flaw was getting over her fears and consistent anxiety. She grew up filled with fear. After experiencing her parents dying, she thought she was next. It just made sense. Everyone she loved died, so why wouldn't she be next in line? For a time, she became too afraid to leave her foster home, to sleep in pure darkness, to talk to other people. She thought the world was out to kill her. Living here, she wasn't exactly wrong with all of the plots the government had against its people. The world *was* out to get her, to put her down as quickly as possible, while taking as much money as possible.

Blair dusted her knees off, wincing at the light sting. She pushed herself to her feet, wobbling a little on her heels before steadying herself. She just had to get home. That was all that she needed to do, and she was just a few feet away from her car. Driving in New York City was no piece of cake, but it was better than being all alone in this creepy parking garage. She gathered herself and her things before heading over to her passenger's side. She unlocked her car with a little beep of her keys before opening the door and placing her purse and phone inside on the seat. She situated her black purse up straight so that it wouldn't topple over while she was driving and spill everywhere. That happened way too many times before.

As she ducked out of her car, she heard a faint noise. At first, it didn't sound familiar to her because it sounded so muffled and a little far away. However, as the seconds ticked by, she realized that the sound was getting closer, and it was coming from behind her. It only took another second for the realization to dawn on her that the sound that she was hearing was footsteps.

CHAPTER FIVE

The last thing that Blair wanted to do was turn around. She just wished that she could somehow melt through the floor or snap her fingers and disappear, but she was just an ordinary human. She had no abilities that could help her right now. Deep down, she knew she needed to turn around. Maybe she was just hearing things, or maybe it was a worker leaving late like her. Her curiosity was starting to grate against her fear, and it eventually won, prompting her to spin around on the spot.

Instead of seeing someone hurry to their car to get back home or seeing no one at all like she had hoped, Blair's eyes fell on a man standing just a few feet away from her. He actually looked a little familiar, but she couldn't place him. Maybe he just had one of those familiar-looking faces. What was strange to her was that he was wearing a black baseball cap that hung low on his head, a black jacket, dark jeans, and black boots. It didn't really seem like office attire or anything like that, so she guessed he was just some random guy. Maybe he was a squatter that slept in the parking garage. She heard of those before.

Silence hung between them for a few seconds, and Blair felt anxiety and awkwardness clash around inside of her, making her feel incredibly uncomfortable. Why wasn't he saying anything? Did she need to say anything? He was the one being creepy approaching her in a poorly lit parking garage.

"Blair Thompson?" the man finally spoke, tilting his head a little at her as his dark eyes surveyed her.

Blair merely nodded, not knowing how to really reply to that. How did he know her name? She wished that she could see more under his cap because he really did seem somewhat familiar. Maybe she'd seen him walking on the street or in the grocery store. Her body tensed up tighter and tighter as the seconds went by, anticipating what was going to happen next. She didn't think that she could probably prepare for it, but she wanted to at least try, despite her fear making her want to act like Jell-O.

"Are you... Do you need something from me?" Blair stumbled over her response, wanting to end this interaction so that she could get in her car and head home. She didn't get paid enough to deal with this.

A smile slowly crept across the man's lips, his shoulders seeming to shake a bit with quiet laughter. "I guess you could say that," he murmured lowly.

Before Blair could even register the flush of fear that shot through her, she heard tires screech behind her. She whipped around to see a black van gun its way up the ramp toward her, making her jump back automatically against the guy. She flinched wildly, her heart hammering against

25

her chest as his arms wrapped around her body, trapping her to him.

"Let me go!" Blair shouted as the van screeched to a stop near her car. She tried to throw her elbow back against the man, striking his abdomen over and over, but he didn't budge. He was far taller and bulkier than her, squeezing her to a point where it hurt. She winced, kicking wildly as he started to drag her back away from her car.

"Come on!" the driver of the van shouted once he rolled down his window, motioning for the man to hurry up. He was older, maybe in his forties, with thin, brown hair and almost honey-colored skin. He slapped the side of his door a few times, the clanging sound echoing throughout the garage.

The side door of the van suddenly slid open, one more man coming into view as he crouched inside. He was masked with a dark jacket and jeans.

"I'm trying!" the man holding Blair grunted, gritting his teeth as he fought against Blair's attempts to escape. He resorted to picking her up, grunts of pain echoing from him as she wildly kicked at his shins.

Blair did the last thing that she could think of doing and threw her head back, feeling the back of it collide with the man's nose.

A cry of pain sounded from him as he stumbled, nearly dropping Blair. Instead, his grip on her grew tighter, his blunt nails digging into her as he yanked her toward the open door of the van.

"Get in there!" he snapped sharply as he tossed Blair down against the hard surface of the van's floor. He scowled at her, lifting his hand to his injured nose before abruptly shutting the door behind her, causing darkness to fall over her.

Blair started to get up off of the floor of the van, but she was pushed down onto her stomach as the man in the back of the van straddled her back, working to tie her hands together behind her back. She kicked and cried out, her throat growing sore with each panicked sound she forced out as loud as she possibly could.

"Stop!" she protested, trying to writhe beneath the man as he secured her hands with a zip tie. She could hardly think straight, panic thundering in her head as she glanced around. Before she knew it, something black covered her eyes, pressure forming on the back of her head. It didn't stop the panicked tears that fled her eyes. She could feel the van moving beneath her, taking her to a place that she didn't know. How did this happen?

Blair tried to calm herself, attempting to breathe normally, but it felt like she was trying to suck air in through a straw. She felt the van take a right turn as her mind tried to capture every detail that she felt and had seen before the blindfold was placed over her eyes.

"Please let me go... I didn't do anything," she whimpered, not speaking to any of the three men specifically. She knew that her pleas wouldn't do anything for her, but she at least wanted them to show her mercy. Did they want money? Did they want government knowledge? She was willing to give them anything they wanted so that she could walk free and stay alive. If she had to up and disappear after this, then she would if it meant keeping herself kicking.

"Shut up back there," the man in the passenger's seat snapped at her, making her whimpers fall silent. He turned back around with a huff, muttering words to the driver that she couldn't hear.

Eventually, the man hovering over her moved off of her to sit elsewhere in the back of the van, leaving her to just lay on the floor on her stomach since she was too afraid to move a muscle.

Blair had no idea why they were so aggressive toward her. She didn't even know them or, at least, didn't think she did. She should've listened to her instincts because she had a feeling that something had been off lately. However, she would've never guessed this to happen in a million years. She didn't think that she'd done anything kidnap worthy, but there she was, all tied up and blindfolded in a van with three strangers.

Dread settled over her, and she knew she was helpless. The only thing she could do was press her forehead down against the floor of the van, squeezing her eyes shut as more tears were absorbed into the fabric of the blindfold. Quietly, she cried, not knowing what was about to happen or if she would even survive it.

CHAPTER SIX

Eventually, the van stopped. Blair opened her eyes, her heart rate jumping back up as she heard the van's doors start to open and shut. She tensed up, feeling the man in the back grip her shoulders to help her to her feet. She felt dizzy as she stumbled around blindly, being led out onto more concrete. She tried to listen for any clues, but it was dead silent besides the men talking to one another. She could be anywhere right now. She'd lost track of how much time passed from when she got in the van until now, so she had no idea how long they drove her for.

"You're going too slow." The driver's voice sounded a few seconds later, being followed with a bruising grip on her forearm. He dragged her forward roughly, making her trip and stumble over her heels again.

Blair gritted her teeth as she tried to regain her balance, anxious breaths puffing from her as they led her into a place that seemed dark, quiet, and cold. She thought that was how the place was anyway. She couldn't exactly tell, but the hairs raising on the back of her neck clued her in a bit. She felt herself being guided down a flight of stairs, her heels clicking on each step. She wondered if they were taking her to a basement or some sort of bunker underground. She didn't remember going up any flights of stairs.

"Over here," one of the men spoke gruffly.

Blair felt the hand on her arm yank her sideways before she was forced to sit down in a plain, wooden chair with thin armrests. She felt the zip tie binding her hands together give way, but the moment of freedom soon disappeared as her wrists were slammed against the armrests. Her wrists were tied to the armrests with thin rope, strapping them down tight. The same thing happened to her ankles, which were tied to the front legs of the chair. She strained her wrists against the rope, trying to pull them free.

Suddenly, a hand struck her cheek, pulling a pained cry from her at the sharp impact. Her bottom lip trembled as she whimpered in pain from her cheek stinging. She stopped struggling, not wanting to be struck again by whoever had hit her. She guessed it was either the driver or the first man. They seemed to be the most aggressive for some reason.

"What now?" A new voice sounded, one that must've belonged to the man in the back of the van with her. He seemed to sound annoyed or overwhelmed.

"We break her down. You know the drill, Koda," the first man replied with a grunt. He reached forward to rip the blindfold off of Blair, who blinked her eyes rapidly against the bright fluorescent light bars hanging above.

"Not really," Koda muttered, his voice coming out faint.

Blair glanced around at her surroundings, taking in the space. It just looked like a concrete room. The only thing in the small room was her chair. It was like this place was meant for keeping people captive, which worried her even more. Who had taken her, and why? She glanced at the first man, still unable to figure out where she'd seen him as the brim of his cap painted shadows across most of his face. The only thing that she could see was a dried-up trail of blood streaking from his nose. She must've broken his nose when she threw her head back.

"Where am I?" she asked, her throat feeling raw as she glanced around again until her eyes landed on the door. She wished she could break free and make a run for it, but they would undoubtedly take her down, and she didn't want to face those consequences. It seemed like one second ago, she was having a sort of normal day at work, and now, she was trapped down in some dungeon without the torture tools. She hoped there weren't any torture tools.

The driver suddenly lurched forward, gripping the front of her blouse roughly to jar her before she could even begin to react. "Did I say you could talk?" he snapped at her, baring his teeth at her like an angered dog as he leaned down close to her.

Blair squeezed her eyes shut, wincing as he came so close. She expected another hit, her cheek still heated and aching from the last one. She could've cried because she was so scared, but she felt like she'd run out of tears at this point. She dared to open her eyes and meet his, staring into a dark abyss of anger and greed.

"Did I?" he snapped again at her, prompting her to quickly shake her head.

"Miles, lay off. Come on." The one named Koda sighed as he pulled off his mask. He drifted his hand over tight curls, smoothing them down as he gazed over at her.

Blair stared at Koda for a few seconds, wondering why someone that looked like him was doing this to her. He was young, maybe a few years older than her, and had smooth, brown skin that looked flawless. His lips were plush, his smile was bright, and his eyes were soft and dark. He was taller than six feet and built muscularly, especially his chest and shoulders. He definitely worked out, and he could surely hurt her if she crossed him. However, he seemed to be the one showing the most mercy, and he was far more built and bigger than the other two men, who were built leaner and shorter.

"Why did you have to bring this one along, Ryan?" Miles groaned, rolling his eyes out of pure annoyance as he stepped back from Blair.

"He had all of the information on her." Ryan, the first man, shrugged before giving Koda a warning glare.

Koda ignored the look, turning to gaze at Blair instead. His expression was hard, but it wasn't as harsh as the other men's.

"Look, let's just continue this tomorrow. I need to go wipe the cameras." Koda sighed as he crossed his arms over his broad chest. He turned away from Blair, giving the other men hard looks that encouraged them to bend to his word.

"We'll get some sleep. She, on the other hand, will not." Miles chuckled, flashing Blair a wicked smirk as he left the room for a few minutes.

"What are you guys doing now? We don't need to do any of your theatrics. We're supposed to warn her, and that's it," Koda told them, his teeth gritting a degree as he grumbled the words. He seemed more irritated with the two men than anything.

"You really don't know how all of this works." Ryan smirked as he shook his head at Koda like he was scolding him for doing something wrong or not knowing something that was plainly simple.

"I don't want to know. We were given specific instructions. I'm just following them," Koda replied, turning to face Ryan and towering over him by a few inches. He narrowed his eyes, his chest lifting and falling drastically in heavy breaths.

"To get our point across, we have to break them down. One good way is exhaustion. You should go get some rest before you experience any, tough guy," Ryan bit out, stepping to the side to give Koda a clear path to the door.

Koda glanced at Blair, his eyes seeming to soften a hint before he looked back at Ryan.

"I'll be back tomorrow. Do not do anything without me," he told Ryan sternly before stepping out of the room, leaving Blair alone with Ryan.

Blair felt dread seep through her as Ryan turned to her, a smirk lining his lips. She wished that Koda was back in here. She didn't like him, because he still helped them kidnap her, but he seemed to keep the other two at bay to not hurt her all that much. She needed some sort of mercy right now, but she knew that she wouldn't receive it from the other two.

"I'm going to go sleep in my nice, comfortable bed. You get to have a party tonight, princess. How about that?" Ryan quipped in a cruel manner as Miles returned with a radio.

Miles set the radio on the floor a few feet away from Blair, a long, orange extension cord running from its short cord and out of the room. He glanced at Ryan, a laugh shaking from him.

"Which station?" Miles asked as he switched on the radio, an announcer's voice rumbling from its two speakers. A soft pop song soon came on, filling the small room with an uplifting tone that had no effect on Blair's sense of gloom and doom.

"Do that metal station." Ryan laughed as he stepped away from Blair.

Miles nodded and turned the dial to the metal station, and loud, thrashing music poured from the speakers. He turned the volume knob up all the way, which hurt Blair's ears as the sound bounced off of the walls.

"Have a nice night, princess!" Ryan shouted to Blair as he and Miles headed out of the room, closing and locking the one door behind them, leaving Blair alone with loud music that already started to make her head throb.

Blair gritted her teeth and shut her eyes, trying to drown out the sound in some way, but nothing worked. It kept pounding against her eardrums relentlessly. As her initial panic started to fade, exhaustion started to take its place. She'd been tossed about, dragged around, and hit all after a long day of work. She was exhausted, wanting to sleep and just escape from this place for at least a few hours. However, they refused to even give her a few hours of peace.

After all of that, Blair still had no idea why she was even in this drastic situation in the first place. It was like they were purposely leaving her hanging just to antagonize her. She suspected that tomorrow would be ten times worse, but she would probably learn the reason she was tied up to a chair in a concrete room. All that she did know was they were supposed to warn her of something, but what could that possibly be? Was it to warn her away from something or to do something?

On top of the noise, the confusion clouding her head just gave her an even worse headache. She was growing so tired that it nearly hurt, discomfort filling her. She drew in a few deep breaths, trying to calm herself, but it was incredibly hard with the heavy thrum of the guitar and the harsh pounding of the drums sounding in the song that was currently playing.

For a few seconds, she found peace once the song ended and the announcer came on to speak. His voice was rough and gruff, but it was a lot quieter than any of the songs playing.

"You're listening to 99.7! Get ready for hard and heavy tunes all night long!" the announcer growled into his microphone, the sound grating against the radio's two old speakers.

"No…" Blair cried the words, dropping her head as another loud song came through the speaker. She shut her eyes, wishing that she was in her bed. She wanted her normal life back, even if she wasn't happy with every aspect of it. She just wanted to go back to it because it was simple in most ways. She could sleep. She wasn't hit. She wasn't kidnapped. How did everything turn upside down so fast? She blinked and things were different. She just wished the next time she opened her eyes that things would be back to normal and she could finally breathe again.

CHAPTER SEVEN

B lair thought that the next day would never come, but it eventually did. She only knew that it came because she heard faint noise from outside of the room. The music had been nonstop, and she hadn't been able to sleep at all. She might've dozed off for a few seconds because she'd been so exhausted that she couldn't help it. However, a loud guitar solo jolted her awake. Now, she felt incredibly drained and hungry. She wanted out of here so badly, but she knew there was no way for her to escape. The rope made her arms and legs sore from being held in one place for so long, and she couldn't break from the rope no matter how hard she pulled against them.

"Good morning!" Ryan announced loudly as he shoved the door open and stepped inside of the room. He slowly moved to the radio and switched it off, drawing a sigh of relief from Blair.

"What? You don't like metal?" Ryan sneered at her as he stepped close to her, tilting his head in a mocking manner as he stared down at her. He wore a security uniform, which was just black cargo pants, black boots, and a black shirt.

Blair gazed up at him, actually seeing his full face now that he wasn't wearing a cap. It suddenly dawned on her why he looked so familiar. He was the security guard that was usually posted at the end of the hallway on her floor at work. She felt her blood run cold at the realization, making her shrink back into the chair that she was tied to.

"Connecting dots, hm?" Ryan commented, watching her lower her head so that she didn't look at him. He didn't seem to like that, finding satisfaction in her grief and anxiety. He gripped her chin, forcing her head up so that their eyes clashed.

"Why are you doing this?" Blair breathed out, her eyes glistening with frightened tears. Things felt scarier now that there were familiar elements involved in all of this. If Ryan was involved in this, she wondered if her department had something to do with her kidnapping. Why would they go through the lengths to do this? Simon was in the office yesterday, and he hadn't said a single word. He only laughed. Was he laughing about this? Did he know about this?

"I would clue you in, but the others aren't here yet. We want to all have a little fun with you." Ryan chuckled, lifting his other hand up to pet at her cheek like she was an animal.

Blair flinched away from his touch as much as she could, but his other hand held her chin firmly in place. She felt her eyes start to gradually narrow, her pain and sadness starting to fade darker and darker. She was starting to feel angry, but it wasn't like she could properly take that anger out on him. She couldn't strike at him, but she could snap at him.

"Don't touch me!" She gritted out, her head starting to feel hotter and hotter. None of this was fair. She wanted out, and her lack of control in this situation just made her more and more irritated. Growing up, she had no control over anything. She couldn't stop her parents from dying. She couldn't stop being mistreated in various foster homes or group homes. She *always* felt powerless.

"What did you just say? Did you just yell at me?" Ryan growled in her face, tightening the hand on her chin like a vice.

"Let me go!" Blair found herself continuing to yell at him, all of the angered thoughts that she had bottled up in her mind finally flowing. She didn't have enough fear to battle that flow. It was far too strong, too directed. When she hit eighteen and was out of the foster care system, she thought that she finally escaped prison, but now, she was right back in it. Her childhood had already been ruined. Was it her adulthood's turn now too?

Ryan struck Blair across the cheek with an open palm, the sound echoing off of the walls and being followed by her pained grunt. The hit was so heavy that Blair accidentally bit her bottom lip, blood welling up from the cut in the tissue.

"Try that again. I dare you," he hissed at her, his tone full of warning as he shook his hand to ward the stinging sensation away.

"Hey, hey, what's going on in here?" Koda's voice soon sounded as he rushed into the room, looking at Ryan with a bewildered look on his face. He looked at Blair, who was grimacing in pain, blood trailing from her lip and down her chin.

"Little brat snapped at me. Had to put her in her place," Ryan muttered as he stepped away from Blair. He shook his head like he was disappointed, rolling his eyes as he turned away from the sight of her.

Koda glanced at Blair with a sigh, lifting his hand to his face to pinch the bridge of his nose. He drew in a breath before meeting her eyes and speaking to her in a quiet tone, which felt like a blessing against her tired ears.

"It's better if you keep silent. There are some things we have to explain to you," Koda told her, his voice firm, but it wasn't a growl or anything. It was like he was just rattling off instructions.

Blair merely looked away, not wanting to listen to a word that they had to say, but she knew that she needed to know why she was even here in the first place. She felt like it had something to do with her work, but she wanted confirmation of that before she started creating theories in her head. It was easy to think up crazy scenarios in her state.

"Left some donuts on the table if you want any," Miles said as he walked into the room to join the others, a glazed donut perched between his fingers as he took a bite of it. He looked like he'd just rolled out of bed, his body adorned in a red and black flannel shirt over a black T-shirt with gray sweatpants and black sneakers.

"Not for you, though," Miles told Blair with a smirk.

Koda rolled his eyes as he crossed his arms, looking at Miles and Ryan.

"I have to get to work soon. Let's get this done."

"You're no fun," Ryan muttered as he stepped forward toward Blair, who shrunk back in her seat again.

Ryan placed his hands over Blair's wrists and leaned down toward her.

"You're here because you're a little snitch," Ryan told her, giving her a hard look.

"A snitch? I haven't said a thing!" Blair blurted out before another slap met her other cheek, snapping her head to the side with force. She gritted her teeth, her eyes watering as she turned back to Ryan with a glare. If she could tear his head off, she would. He was lucky that she was restrained. She learned how to throw a punch in one of her group homes, and he didn't want to be on the other end of that.

"You've been acting suspicious. Simon has been alerted to your odd behavior lately. Since you deal with highly classified information, he can't take risks if you're thinking of revealing secrets. This is your warning," Ryan growled at her, pulling out all the stops to intimidate her.

Blair knew that she hadn't been acting like a complete model employee lately with her slow work and glaring at the camera, but she didn't think that they would flag something like that. Sure, she'd been thinking certain thoughts of exposing government secrets, but she hadn't even made a move to do so. Plus, this was a warning? This felt like punishment for something that she hadn't even done yet.

"Now, you're going to be in timeout for a little bit just to make sure you don't go flapping your mouth. Don't worry, we'll have a grand old time together." Ryan smirked as he stood up and stepped back from her.

"I haven't done anything. I haven't told anyone anything." Blair stressed to them, hoping that they would just realize that this was one big mistake and that they would let her go. However, she was probably already too far in, and they were far too happy about antagonizing her for that to happen. She knew where Ryan came from, but she wondered where Koda and Miles came from. It sounded like Koda worked for the government, but she wasn't so sure about Miles. She knew nothing about the three of them except for Ryan being a security guard for her floor.

"Maybe you have. Maybe you haven't. We don't know what you might be planning for the future, though. You came from nothing. You'd be someone to blabber," Miles told her before popping the last bite of his donut into his mouth to chew on.

Blair narrowed her eyes at his words, feeling them strike deep within her for some reason. She didn't come from nothing. She came from her parents, who were good people. Her father was in the military, and her mother worked in a factory. They passed when she was twelve, and she missed them every single day of her life. They didn't deserve what happened to them.

"How would I be someone to blabber?" she bit out, wondering what he meant by that. If he knew what she found out the government was up to, he would want to blabber too if he was a decent person. Then again, he didn't seem to be a good person at all. She could tell that much about him.

"You're one of those people who probably feel wronged by the world. You blabber theories and secrets. Stuff that isn't yours to tell so that people feel sorry for you," Miles replied with a bit of a bite in his tone as he glared at her from across the room.

"Alright, alright. I think we're done here for today." Koda sighed, turning to Miles to give him a look that told him to shut his mouth.

"Guess I'll go eat another donut. Hungry?" Miles asked Blair with a sneer before heading out of the room.

Blair shifted in the chair, the discomfort feeling nearly so harsh that it made her eyes water. She'd never felt so uncomfortable in her own skin before in her life. She was so tired, sore, and hungry that she could hardly stand it. She wanted sleep the most, though. She just hoped that they would all leave soon so that she could catch an hour or two of rest at least. It would give her enough energy to try to cope with all of this.

"Want some tunes, princess?" Ryan laughed out before turning the radio on again, blasting more metal music in the room. He gave her a crude wink before leaving the room.

Blair shut her eyes and shook her head, drawing in a shaky breath as she realized that she would face another night of no sleep. She couldn't go on much longer like this. It was so painful and uncomfortable.

Koda gazed at Blair with a seemingly blank look on his face. He glanced at the door briefly, seeming to wait for a few minutes before he stepped forward and shut the radio off, silence falling on the room. He even went so far as to unplug the radio too, sliding the radio to the side of the room with his black dress shoe.

Blair's eyes slowly opened, confusion gracing her face as she looked up at Koda, who stood there in what looked like a gray work suit. She wondered why exactly he did that. She refused to think that he was a good person since he was involved with all of this. He had to have done that for some other ulterior motive that just wasn't clear to her yet. Her eyes trailed him as he left the room without a word, shutting and locking the door behind him. She was left with silence.

Blair could've cheered whilst a heavy sigh of relief burst from her as she leaned back in the wooden chair. She could actually try to sleep now until they came back. She wasn't sure how Miles and Ryan would react to the radio being off, but that was Koda's doing, not hers. They could take it out on him. She was just going to take advantage of this moment and get some rest. She needed the clarity to think her way out of this because it was all turning into a deep, red haze. She wasn't sure how much longer she could fight off what was boiling inside of her. Maybe it wouldn't be a bad idea to release it now. It might be the only thing that decided whether she made it out of this or not.

CHAPTER EIGHT

At this point, Blair didn't know how many days she'd been in the concrete room. It could've been three or four, but she wasn't really sure. She was approaching her breaking point, though. She knew that much. She felt humiliated, being pushed around by mainly Miles and Ryan in an effort to "break her down". She suspected that she was getting close to that point because she felt on the verge of death. She'd only slept a few hours, eaten probably a small sleeve of saltine crackers, and drank maybe two cups of water. She felt like her body wanted to shut down forever, and she couldn't blame it. Her mind was exhausted too, ready to give up.

She suspected that she would be worse off if Koda didn't step in as often as he did. When the other two were hitting on her or being too rough, he stepped in, forcing them away from her to allow her to recover. She didn't know why he acted like that, like he was trying to be the nice one, like he was trying to save her. He wasn't saving her, because she was still stuck to the chair in that room. Sitting there hadn't helped her attitude. She had plenty of time to stew in her thoughts, to be reminded of all of the unfair things that happened to her throughout her life. It was hard to do anything else in there besides think, which wasn't a really great thing for her to do. All she could think about were the bad things that happened to innocent people.

Deep down, Blair almost wished that she *had* spilled some secrets. At least she wouldn't be in this situation for nothing. She would've at least informed some people before being stuck in here. She would rather be in prison at this point. She would actually get three meals a day and be allowed to sleep properly there at least. She felt like they were playing with her here, trying to antagonize her as much as possible. She didn't even know what would happen once they broke her down. Would she be released? Maybe she should just go ahead and give up, but she had a bad feeling. She had no clue what would happen, and she wasn't sure if she wanted to find out.

Her stomach growled painfully, and her teeth gritted as she leaned over as much as she possibly could, trying to quell the ache. She'd been hungry before back in her youth, but she'd never been hungry like this. The crackers that she'd gotten kept her from dying, but they didn't sate her hunger at all. Even when she heard the door open, she didn't look up, just wanting to curl up as much as she could.

"Brought you some water." Koda's voice sounded from across the room. He approached her, despite her not moving to look up, holding a plastic cup of water in his hand. He awkwardly stood in front of her, waiting for her to look up.

Blair gritted her teeth, hating that other people got to see her looking like this. She felt so weak, and she hated feeling weak, useless, hopeless. It grated on her nerves, amplified the darkness that she harbored since she was younger. There was no getting rid of it. She could only try to quash and control it, but that was an impossible feat in here. There were too many things to be upset about, and they were all linked to the government that she worked for. It was so corrupt that it tried to silence people who breathed weird. It wasn't fair. How could the government expect her to trust them if they didn't have an ounce of trust in her? She refused to give them any more satisfaction, to bow down.

"Go away." She found herself gritting, wanting him to just go away. She didn't care about the mercy that he showed her. It had to be a trick, a way to get her to trust him so that she would break faster. She wasn't going to play his game or fall for his tricks. She would figure a way out, or she would die in here being silent. She didn't want to break, despite it seeming like a form of relief for her at this point.

"Drink. You need it." Koda tried to prompt her, holding the plastic cup forward a little.

Blair shook her head before lifting her eyes to his. She glared at him, warning him to back off quietly. She wanted to be alone. She didn't want him around her spouting his lies. She was tired of hearing any of them.

"Look, I know that this sucks, but you have to take care of yourself as much as you can." Koda sighed, giving her a softer look, trying to convince her to just drink the water.

Blair rolled her eyes, deciding to play with him like they played with her. It was only fair that she got a few hits in.

"Fine, a few sips." She sighed, softening her expression. She leaned forward as he brought the cup toward her, her lips settling on the rim as he tilted the cup a little. The cold water felt like paradise, but she didn't let him know that. She took a few sips, but she bottled them up in the hollow of her cheeks. Once he brought the cup away, she spat the water at him.

"Really!" Koda growled as he jumped back away from her, gazing down at the wet spots on his white button-down. He shook his head as he turned to place the cup down on the floor, grumbling beneath his breath.

"I told you to leave me alone. I don't want your fake help," Blair spat at him, turning her nose up with a roll of her eyes. It actually irritated her more that he was trying to act like a good guy because it couldn't be genuine. If he were actually a nice guy, he would have let her out by now, but she was still stuck here.

"Fake help? Are you serious?" Koda asked, narrowing his eyes at her as he stepped closer to her. He towered over her, his shadow falling against her. He was intimidating, but she had a feeling that he wouldn't hurt her. He didn't seem like the type to lash out like that, but she couldn't trust anyone at this point.

"You're just trying to play good cop so that I'll trust you. I'm calling your bluff. You're just as bad as the others," Blair muttered, shaking her head. He might not have been as outwardly harsh as Ryan and Miles, but he had the same end goal. He was just as bad.

Koda was silent for a few seconds before sighing, seeming to slowly deflate from his tense state. "You know that's not true. I'm not as bad as them," Koda murmured quietly, his shoulders slumping a little as he glanced toward the ground.

Blair kept her eyes narrowed, not wanting to lower her guard. She couldn't trust him, like she couldn't trust the others. Her own department had betrayed her, but she supposed that she had the mentality to betray them as well. However, they were doing things that were corrupt and evil. She wanted to service the public, to warn them of things that they probably already suspected, but they needed proof. She wanted to give them proof, and there were plenty of instances that she could show them.

"Don't act like this. The others won't tolerate it. They're not as merciful as me." Koda warned her, his voice dipping down low, like he was sharing a secret with her. He glanced toward the door, like he expected the others to burst in and prove his point right.

Blair followed his eyes, tensing up a degree before convincing herself to relax. He was just trying to rile her up, and she didn't need to let him under her skin. That was exactly where he wanted to place himself.

"I'm pretty tired. Could you leave?" Blair asked, lowering her eyes to the tips of her heels. She hadn't been able to take them off yet, and they were killing her feet. However, she hadn't dared to mention it to anyone. Miles and Ryan would probably duct tape them to her feet, while Koda would try to act nice and take them off for her. It would be nice to have them off, but she wasn't going to let him do anything nice if she couldn't help it.

"Do you need anything else before I leave?" Koda sighed, seeming to give up and just prepare to leave for the day. It was obvious that he wasn't going to get anywhere with her right now.

"Nope," Blair replied a second later, popping her lips. She just needed him to leave before her discomfort took hold and made her accept favors. It was getting harder and harder with each day, but she needed to hold strong. She owed that to all of the people that the government was taking advantage of. If she could just be strong and figure a way out, she would be someone that she could be proud of. She wanted to be stronger than she used to be, and she could only do that by keeping her head up and forging through this. She just had to take it one breath at a time.

CHAPTER NINE

The lull of Miles' and Ryan's voices faded into the background of Blair's thoughts. It was another day, meaning another time for Miles and Ryan to annoy her. They weren't hitting her as much, but if she got an attitude, they were sure to shove her around or strike her. She resorted to not saying anything, but they refused to leave. They just wanted to be obnoxious and annoy her, so they started playing cards on the floor in front of her.

"Hope we're not bothering you, princess," Ryan quipped with a laugh before slapping a card down on the concrete floor.

An aggravated curse broke from Miles as he slammed his cards down.

Blair ignored them, wondering what time it was currently. Everything started to blur together at a point since she hadn't seen the sun in days. She missed feeling the sunshine on her skin and watching the rain out of her apartment window. She missed so many small things that she felt she hadn't appreciated enough. She wondered if she would ever experience them again. They hit the jackpot kidnapping her because no one cared about her.

She had no family expecting her. Her friends rarely saw or heard from her anyway. She was a perfect, lone target.

"Hey, at least you're not having to work," Ryan told Blair, constantly making comments and pitching looks over at her while he and Miles played another round. He continued to antagonize her, wanting to break her down, to reduce her to tears, begging, and swearing that she'd never say anything.

Blair had a feeling that no matter what happened after she got out of there, if she ever did, that nothing would ever be the same. She would either be trailed every minute of every day or banished to the middle of nowhere. Maybe she would be killed. It was hard to conjure up much hope nowadays, but she just focused on her goal. She'd been helpless many times during her life, but other people didn't have to be if she could try to help it. If she was going to die, it was going to be for a good reason. She wanted to have some sort of impact on the world.

For so long, she believed that her life would never have any impact. After years and years of feeling sorry for herself, she finally realized that she could have an impact if she really tried. She just had to look past her own emotions and be brave. It was all about being brave, which was the hardest obstacle for her to face.

"You should probably just let me go. I'm not giving in to anything," Blair muttered, hoping that they would take the hint and release her to fend for herself. She would leave the country if she had to, and that honestly didn't sound like a bad idea at some points. This country was a mess anyway.

"Oh, no, no. I need to make sure that you won't even breathe a word of anything that you've seen. I can't let you go if I'm not sure," Ryan replied with a shake of his head.

"You're just a security guard. I don't even know what you are. What are you getting out of this?" Blair snapped at them, wondering what they got for doing this to her. What did the government possibly bribe them with? They spent so much time antagonizing her, poking at every weak spot that they could find. It tired her out incredibly, and it had to be tiring at least a little bit to them too at this point. It had to have been close to a week since she was brought in here. It honestly felt like a few months at this point.

"A damn good paycheck." Miles chuckled, sharing a pleased look with Ryan.

"Miles provided this lovely venue. It's gotten quite a few good uses," Ryan explained to her, motioning to the space that she was trapped in.

Blair felt a cold rush flow through her at his words, shifting her eyes around. She wondered how many people had been trapped in here before her and how many would be trapped here after. It was literally a room built for kidnap victims that was rented out by the government. What kind of world did she live in? She wanted to leave as soon as possible.

"That's right. You're not the first, honey. Don't feel special," Miles commented, noticing Blair's bewildered look. He shuffled the cards between his hands, letting them shift and filter between his fingers and palms to mix them up.

"I just can't believe you're so shallow that money justifies torturing people to you," Blair replied within a mutter, her nails digging into her palms as laughter bubbled from the other men. It annoyed her that they laughed at everything she said, like they were ridiculing her. They should know that they were awful people, but they just didn't care. She couldn't change the mindsets or opinions of people who didn't care what people thought of them in the first place.

"Money runs the world. Haven't you learned that by now?" Ryan asked her with a tilt of his head. He smirked a little before nudging Miles and standing up.

"We should go meet the boss and get our pay anyway. Hang in there, princess," Ryan told Miles before turning to Blair and winking.

Blair watched them walk out of the room, the lights in the room suddenly shutting off, drowning her in darkness. They hadn't done that before. She shifted around nervously, not being a big fan of the dark. She didn't like being unable to see what was in front of her. What if something was there somehow? She wouldn't even have a clue. Darkness felt so heavy to her, weighing down on her shoulders and on her mind. It made her feel even more alone at this point, making her sink further down into her thoughts.

Money. It all came down to money. A lot of the motivation behind the government's actions was also money. It made people do awful things, and it was the ultimate motivator, besides someone's own life, at the end of the day. She understood being motivated by money because she went through a lot of lengths to earn money, but that was so she could live a semi-comfortable life and afford her rent and bills. She needed it mainly for survival, while having a few bucks left over for something fun. Money was linked to living for her. She wouldn't want to put money above the lives of other people, though.

Blair knew what it was like to be last choice. She knew what it was like to be treated like nothing, and she just couldn't see herself treating innocent people like that. The pain of experiencing that herself still stuck with her, paining her in a way. She didn't want to pass on that pain, to have it spread like sickness. She would rather suffer with it herself because she didn't want others to go through such feelings.

She wanted to stand with the people, who were more genuine and real than the government that ruled over them. Even if she wasn't treated all that great growing up, it didn't match up to the amount of silent abuse that was inflicted on everyone else. It needed to end, and change started with information. She knew where all of the information was located. All she had to do was escape from here and release it all to the rest of the world. Even if she was taken out after that moment, the people could take the next step. They could run with her sacrifice and change the world because that was the entire point of all of this.

KIDNAPPED

CHAPTER TEN

The first thing that Blair noticed was the smell of bacon. It was a smell that she felt she hadn't come across in months, but she could smell it now. She blinked her eyes open slowly as she heard the door to the concrete room creak open, the lights in the room flickering back on. Once her eyes adjusted, she watched Koda step inside of the room before shutting the door behind him. He had a white, plastic bag in one hand as he slowly approached Blair.

"You were MIA yesterday," Blair muttered, having dealt with only Miles and Ryan yesterday as they played about a million card games. Even if he was being a fake, Blair preferred Koda's company because he was far quieter and less rude to her. Plus, he never laid a hand on her. At this point, she felt like her face was constantly bruised and her lips were constantly split from all of the hits that she endured lately. She just couldn't help but make snappy comments, having lost her nervous edge to the darker side of her that she tried to hide. She felt safer being harsh too, like it gave her some sort of protection that her usual nervous attitude couldn't.

"I had work," Koda replied as he pulled out something in a white wrapper from the plastic bag. He unwrapped the top to reveal what looked like a breakfast sandwich. That was what it smelled like to Blair.

In direct response, Blair's stomach growled loudly, making her glance away out of embarrassment. Her body continually betrayed her. Every time her stomach growled around Miles and Ryan, they made it a point to grab food, bring it down to the concrete room, and then eat in front of her, plainly taunting her. That stung because her hunger was only getting worse and worse. It weakened her in so many ways, but she fought through. She focused on the end goal.

"What is work for you?" Blair asked him, trying to continue with the subject so that they could just ignore her body crying for the food in his hand. She didn't want to beg, and she felt so afraid that he was going to bait her with the sandwich or make her plead for it. She wouldn't do that, but it would wear on her terribly.

"I guess like HR. I compile employee information and such," Koda replied casually as he stepped up closer to her. He glanced at the sandwich and then back at her, a sense of awkwardness developing between them that was accompanied by a brief silence. "I got you breakfast. I figured those idiots didn't feed you yesterday," Koda muttered, shaking his head a little as he extended his hand out with the sandwich toward her.

Blair really didn't like being fed by someone else's hand, but what other choice did she have? She shifted forward a little, preparing to take a bite, but she suddenly froze. What if the sandwich was poisoned or laced with something that would knock her out or make her less in control of her actions? She eyed the sandwich suspiciously, glancing at each layer of cheese, egg, and bacon, like she expected to see whatever drug dripping from it.

"I didn't do anything to it," Koda told her, something close to a small smile quirking up on his lips. He seemed a little amused as she studied the sandwich so adamantly. After a moment, he sighed and lifted the sandwich and took a bite out of it. He chewed on it steadily before swallowing and extending his hands in a motion of showmanship.

"See? I hate my life right now, but I don't hate it that much to poison myself with a breakfast sandwich." Koda sighed before extending the sandwich back out to her, shifting the side around so that she could bite into the other side.

Blair felt a brief flicker of amusement flare up within her, but she quelled it immediately. She didn't want to joke with this man. However, since there wasn't a catch with this sandwich, she was going to eat it and collect her strength. She leaned forward and took a bite, nearly feeling like she could cry at the taste. It was the first meal-like food that she'd eaten in like a week, and it felt like the best thing she'd ever tasted in her entire life. She knew that probably wasn't the case, but hunger did a number to her brain. Brussels sprouts seemed like a gourmet dish at this point, and she hated brussels sprouts.

"I didn't know what you liked, so I just chose something," Koda murmured as he pulled the sandwich back to let her chew. He seemed awkward standing there, but he stood his ground, continuing to let her take bites of the sandwich.

"I'd eat anything at this point," Blair muttered, chewing slowly on the buttery biscuit part. She didn't know when the next time would be that she ate something as good as this again. She had learned to appreciate small things like this now. She wished that she had done that before all of this, but she just tried to do it now.

"I am sorry about them. They kind of take things to the extreme," Koda told her, a sort of guilty look crossing his face as he shifted on the spot.

Taking things to the extreme didn't even cover the things that they put her through. They were evil people. What else could she expect from people like them? It was odd to hear an apology when she was in such a predicament, which made it seem less worthy to her. If he was sorry, he really didn't show it all that much. Sure, feeding her and not beating her were technically nice things to do, but it didn't make up for the fact that he helped them do this to her.

Plus, it seemed like he worked in the same building as her, except he was in the HR department. He dug up her information to help with this whole scheme, and she didn't even care that he sounded like he didn't want to be a part of this, because he still was. He was still a factor.

"I told you that I didn't do anything. I don't understand why that isn't enough to just let me go." Blair gritted between slow chews. It was hard to be angry while eating, but she felt like she was still pulling it off. What also made it hard was when she made sharp comments, it was like she was staring at a kicked puppy. Koda seemed so deflated when she spoke to him like that, but she couldn't bring herself to be nice to him. He was at fault for her even being here. She had a right to be mad, and she was going to exercise that right. The government hardly allowed her or anyone else to exercise any other rights anyway.

"It's just Simon and the other heads. They want to be sure that you're too scared to say anything ever. Miles and Ryan have broken people before because they're so ruthless, so Simon hired them on again for you," Koda explained before crumbling up the empty, white wrapper and tucking it into the plastic bag. He tossed the bag near the door before turning back to her, steadily crossing his arms over his chest as he gazed at her.

"How nice of them. They have some trust issues, don't they?" Blair commented, her tone full of sarcasm. She was irritated, but she couldn't change her government. She could ruin them, though. They deserved it anyway as they lined their pockets with the money of people that actually needed it. It was despicable, but there was a lot of dirt on them. They were a walking time bomb that was bound to blow up at any second if one wrong thing slipped out.

Koda was quiet for a few seconds, a more curious look creeping onto his face as he tilted his head at her a little. "Your observations in your report made you seem pretty shy and soft-spoken. You don't seem to be those things," he commented with an intrigued tone.

Blair narrowed her eyes a little, feeling like she was being scrutinized and studied like a lab animal. She hadn't realized that her employee profile was full of observations, which she didn't even know or want to know what those entailed and who did the observing, and she didn't like how it seemed as if Koda studied her profile or something. She felt violated in a way, but the government was the most violating being there was in the country. She should've expected something like this, but it still sickened her that it was confirmed like it was no big deal.

"My observations didn't report you to be a creep, but I guess I was wrong," Blair commented sharply, shifting her eyes away from him. She didn't like feeling his eyes on her. She felt like he was picking apart every piece of her, like she was a toy to play with and assemble. Didn't he know that what he was doing was strange and wrong?

Koda blinked a few times at her words, looking stung, like he'd just gotten slapped in the face. If Blair's wrists weren't still tied down to the chair, he would've expected her to lash out at him. He stared at her for a few seconds, eyeing her steely expression before sighing and turning around to put his back to her. He headed for the door and leaned down to grab the empty bag, pausing once his hand gripped the doorknob. Seeming to fight himself, he hurriedly opened the door and left the room, letting the door swing shut behind him, and the sound of a lock clicking soon followed.

"Good. Creep," Blair muttered as she slumped back in her chair. She felt proud and accomplished for a few seconds before the image of his hurt face popped into her head. She tried to push it away, but it stuck with her. It was hard to be mean to someone with a soft face like his. It was even harder because he wasn't really mean to her in any way. It was like being mean to a puppy.

Blair felt her hard expression soften gradually, a faint sigh breaking from her. It was weird having someone act so nice to her, which confused her. She couldn't really tell if he was faking or not. Her defensive instincts were waving red flags, but another part of her tried to convince herself that he was a decent person stuck in a bad situation like her. Maybe he didn't have a choice in the matter, and he had to help the others kidnap her. Maybe he was just as bad as the others. Maybe she was going crazy. It wasn't the strangest possibility at this point.

CHAPTER ELEVEN

"Guilty. Guilty!"

Blair jolted awake with a soft gasp, shooting her eyes open as Ryan and Miles suddenly burst into the room. She blinked away the sleepy haze in her eyes so that she could properly see them, wondering why they were bursting into the room so suddenly and so early. What had they said?

"What?" Blair muttered, having missed the obnoxious yelling that Ryan spouted off before entering the room. She tightened her fingers into fists as they approached, standing over her with wicked grins that made her blood run cold. She felt like maybe she didn't want to hear whatever they said.

"Guilty," Miles repeated Ryan's words to her.

Blair narrowed her eyes, wondering what they meant by calling her guilty. As far as she knew, she wasn't guilty of anything but being moronic enough to accept her current job position. Honestly, at this point, she wasn't even sure if she was employed at the moment. Regardless, she was probably going to quit anyway and find something else that didn't make her skin crawl.

"Of what?" she asked as they stood on either side of her. She knew that they were just doing that to intimidate her. Truthfully, it didn't make her feel all that great or safe, but she clenched her jaw and tried to put on a tough face. That was all that she could do at this point anyway since she couldn't even budge.

"We heard a tip that they're collecting evidence against you. So what did you say? Who did you tell?" Ryan asked, leaning close to her like she was going to exchange a secret with him.

Blair leaned away as much as she could, a bewildered look crossing her face at his words. Why were they collecting evidence? They wouldn't find anything on her, because she hadn't done anything besides glare at a camera. She zoned out. That wasn't her fault hardly. She felt like they were grabbing at the air at this point, trying to pull something out that looked like evidence. They were getting desperate, and that worried her. Bad things happened when people were desperate.

"I didn't tell anyone anything," Blair told them for what felt like the hundredth time since she had gotten there. She wished they would get that through their thick skulls, but it never seemed to work. As they crowded her, already getting close to touching her, she felt her mind drift to Koda and how she actually wished he were there right then. He would get these two to back off of her, but he was nowhere to be found.

Lately, Ryan and Miles came together, while Koda came alone. She had a strange feeling that Ryan and Miles came to see her when Koda wasn't there or had work. They knew that Koda would hit the brakes on whatever crazy thing they tried to do.

"Oh, come on. Stop lying," Miles groaned, pushing roughly at her shoulder when she didn't immediately reply.

"What did you say?" Ryan backed up Miles, reaching his hand over to rest on the back of the base of her neck, adopting a tight grip.

Blair questioned if she should just make up something that wasn't too incriminating just to get them off of her back, but she knew they would just want more and more from her if she opened that door. Her best defense against those two was silence and ignorance. She didn't need to feed into their negative energy, which threatened to consume her at this point.

"Nothing!" she snapped, getting fed up with their accusatory remarks toward her. She didn't get their fascination with something that wasn't even true.

Ryan shoved his hand up her neck into the tangled black strands of her hair, his fist tightening into a tight grip around her hair. He jerked her hair back so that she was forced to look up at him right into his eyes.

"You're a liar! The report is coming out soon anyway, so you might as well tell us," he growled in her face, making her flinch due to the sharpness of his tone.

"There won't be anything to report on!" Blair gritted out the words, trying to fight past the stinging sensation that she felt in her scalp as he continued to pull on her hair. She wished that they weren't so nosy and awful, inflicting pain on her just to punish her for not spilling every little thing that they wanted to know. They acted like children, throwing fits when they didn't get their way.

Blair knew that she couldn't involve children in her life. She felt like she was tainted, unable to provide her own children a good life growing up because she experienced such an awful one. She didn't have enough experience with the proper raising of children, and she was petrified that she would scar them as badly as she was, like she would mess them up. She didn't want to risk that, not wanting to inflict such ill promise on such an innocent human being. She would feel evil if she hurt their feelings or led them wrong. Parenting seemed like a job that she couldn't make any mistakes doing, and she didn't have any confidence in herself in that realm. Besides, it hardly looked like she would get out of there to have children in the first place.

"I'm guessing she told an old boyfriend or something," Miles commented to Ryan, who smirked and shrugged his shoulders in response.

"Maybe. I don't think this firecracker ever had a boyfriend, though. Koda's file didn't have anything in the relationship tab," Ryan replied with an amused chuckle.

Blair felt her face burn up with embarrassment, shooting her eyes down as laughter surrounded her. How much information about her was in those files? It sounded like it touched on every detail of her life, including the fact that she'd never been with someone before. She was too afraid to, unable to really come around to trusting people in that way. She'd been let down so many times that she was terrified to take the leap. She needed somebody that understood and listened to her.

Plus, she didn't know how to flirt or properly interact with other people. She was either too awkward to interact with them or mean to them. There was a list of issues she knew she needed to deal with, especially when it came to interacting with other people, but ensuring she had a place to live in was more important than attempting to fix her broken brain. She tried to act sociable and kind, but it was like pulling teeth with her. She didn't know how to talk with people, and it made her suffer at times because she really had no one to have her back. Her "friends" were just people that she was able to muster up greetings and casual conversations about the weather with every once in a while.

"Who was it? Mom? Dad? Oh, wait, they're dead." Ryan cackled loudly, Miles' laughter intermingling with his own.

Blair felt the burn of embarrassment ignite into a searing of anger. She couldn't believe that they had the audacity to talk about her parents like that to her. They were working to get under her skin, and that was a quick way to do so. It dug deep inside of her, striking the emotions that were the most raw and sensitive. Even this far into the future, she still grieved for her parents. What child wouldn't if they were close to their parents? At times, she would cry over them, wishing that they'd gotten more time together. She felt like so much time and so many memories with them had been stolen from her, and she never felt like it was right or justified.

"Oh, sorry, did I hit a nerve?" Ryan asked, using a baby-like voice that made her narrow her eyes and clench her jaw.

Blair pleaded herself not to say anything, to keep bottling up her emotions so that nothing came spilling out. She didn't need to give them the satisfaction because all that they wanted out of her was a reaction. She couldn't give them one, no matter how hurt or angry she felt over their words. She merely stared at the tips of her heels, ignoring them as they leaned close, laughing in her ear and nudging her over and over again. She let them poke and prod at her, focusing on her own breathing as it entered in and out of her nose.

Before she even saw it coming, a hand collided with her cheek, jarring her out of her concentration, a shocked look exploding across her face. She looked up at Miles, who gave her an annoyed look. She must've not entertained them enough.

"You're going to wish that Koda was here," Miles told her, the tone of the room seeming to darken quite quickly.

Blair felt the air in her lungs get trapped in there, refusing to leave as she heard someone's knuckles crack. She angered them by refusing to put on a show, by not becoming the spectacle they wanted to laugh at and antagonize. Even when she thought she did something right, it always turned out to be very wrong. The world was upside down and twisted, but she lived in it. There was no escaping it, and there was no escaping the pain that was about to rain down on her.

CHAPTER TWELVE

"**B**lair? Hey! Blair!"

White noise seemed to fill Blair's head, screaming loudly between her ears for a few seconds as the dark world around her turned blurry. It hurt to open her eyes, but she managed to do it anyway, wanting to see the source that was calling her name. She blinked a few times, letting the haziness sharpen to the point where she could make out Koda's worried face.

"Hm?" Blair murmured, feeling like she was moving in slow motion. Her senses seemed to lag, an ache thundering through her head.

"Are you okay?" Koda asked her, one hand lifting to lightly drift his fingertips along the swelling around her left eye. There was a cut on her cheek from someone's ring catching her face, along with the usual split in her bottom lip. She looked broken and beaten, appearing way worse than before.

Blair sighed softly as the white noise finally faded, and she could properly see. She guessed that she'd been knocked out cold or had passed out. Regardless, she preferred the quiet darkness as opposed to being conscious right now. She could use quite a few painkillers, but she wasn't going to be gifted with anything like that in this torture chamber. She must've really pissed off Miles and Ryan, or they had a rough day because they really laid into her that time. They were sorry men with sorry motives.

"Why?" She found herself breathing out weakly, trying to ignore how hot and swollen some parts of her face felt due to being struck so hard. She figured she looked a mess. Her makeup was probably smeared, mixing with the bruises and blood. What a look.

"Why what?" Koda asked her, his eyes narrowing a bit in confusion at her sudden question.

"Why shouldn't I tell people the truth about everything? Isn't that a form of justice for them, to know who is behind everything?" Blair murmured, wondering to herself why she was talking to him about this, but who else was she going to talk to? He was the only one around here who was willing to have an actual conversation with her. She just hadn't taken him up on his offer until now. Besides, later was better than never. She was just curious on his take of the subject since she felt like his opinion would be different from Miles and Ryan's.

Koda drifted a hand over his short hair as he thought for a few moments, weighing his words before speaking them aloud. "It's just safer for them not to know. Do you know what will happen if people found out everything that the government is doing, like had actual proof?" Koda asked her, his eyes seeming to widen just at the thought of it.

Blair didn't understand where he was coming from or why it would be a bad thing for people to find out. They deserved the truth. Didn't he realize that, or was he just brainwashed? He seemed like a smart guy, but the words coming out of his mouth didn't seem so intelligent.

"They would take action and get justice against a government that has wronged them for years. You know the corruption that goes on!" Blair told him, shaking her head a little at him. She expected a revolution, a fight for change that should've happened years ago. However, it was hard to fight against an unfair system that just took and took from the people, leaving them with nothing or threatening to take away what they had left. It was unfair, but the people had the numbers, and they would soon have the ultimate motivation of solid proof. That would be very hard for people to ignore. It was easy to turn a blind eye when there really wasn't anything clear to see.

Koda sighed softly, turning to pace slowly around the room. "There will be riots, maybe even war. Do you know how many people would get killed because of uprisings like that? It wouldn't be safe! Innocents would just get caught in the crossfire of it all," Koda argued with her, an expression of worry crossing his face.

"Innocents are being killed now by the government. Can't you see that? They put so many chemicals in our food, our water, our medicine. They make going to the doctor put you in debt. Too many people are already dying.

They're just good at covering it up." Blair pointed out, remembering all of the messages and files that she sent from department to department. It was all a corrupt web, a system of deception. She couldn't believe that everyone was caught in it like they were. It would be hard to break free.

"Look, I know that what you think you're doing is a good thing, but the aftermath will be catastrophic. You can't try to change a whole country overnight like that," Koda murmured softly as he approached her, his expression seeming to beg her to listen.

Blair was aware that change couldn't happen overnight. It would be a long and hard process, but it had to be better than living like this. They were living in a nightmare disguised as a dream. Bad things were happening every minute, but it was all disguised under so many lies. She just wanted to pull back the curtain for everyone, to give them an inside look at the workings of the country. She didn't know exactly what would happen next, but she hoped that it was change.

It was strange that Koda seemed to care about people but seemed to be going about it in a way that she didn't fully agree with. She knew that people would get hurt and maybe killed as a result of revealing these secrets, but everything would be out in the open. Nothing would be hidden. She sighed softly, knowing that this conversation would go nowhere. They were on two different sides, and her head hurt too badly to argue right now. She would rather talk about something less strenuous on her mind.

"What time is it?" Blair asked him, wondering if it was early in the day or later. She just could never tell, feeling like she was in an endless cycle of fluorescent light with the occasional blackout.

"It's one in the afternoon on a Saturday," Koda told her after checking his phone and then shoving it back into the side pocket of his black joggers.

That explained why he was wearing casual clothes of a red T-shirt and black joggers with black sneakers today. She liked the weekend. Those were the two days that she was free from work and got to go do whatever she wanted with the money that was left over from her paychecks. She mostly just ate out, went to the mall and other stores, and visited local parks and such. She did things that she used to not be able to do regularly. Lately, she'd been eyeing a local volunteer agency, figuring she could try to help on a small-scale level in hopes to level out the bad work that she was doing.

"Right now, I would be eating at Orchid Delight." Blair sighed wistfully, wishing she could eat a full meal right now. It felt like ages since she'd eaten something like that. She would've appreciated her chicken salad sandwiches more if she'd known that this was going to happen to her.

"That Indian place on the corner of Edgewater?" Koda asked with a small tilt of his head, familiarity glinting in his eyes.

Blair nodded, having visited that place more times than she could count. It was owned by a local family, who did all of the cooking, serving, and managing. It tasted authentic too, bringing her back over and over.

"That's the one. I'm a regular," Blair told him, figuring she acquired that title at this point. She went pretty much once every week just to quench her constant craving of it and to support a local business. The family was so kind to her that she tried to help in any way that she could.

"I'll have to check it out. I'm more of a Korean barbeque guy," Koda explained with a faint smile as he tapped away on his phone for a few seconds.

Blair wasn't familiar with the cuisine, but it sounded interesting. She missed trying new things. Things were all the same day to day, and she was growing tired of the repetition. It was like being back in the group homes. A throb echoed through her head, making her wince, her eyes shutting tightly briefly.

"Can't stand these headaches," she muttered to herself, her eyes eventually fluttering back open.

"I'll be right back," Koda suddenly told her before leaving the room, leaving her sitting there with a confused look on her face.

What was he up to now? She wondered if money motivated him to do this like it had the others. He didn't seem particularly money hungry. He seemed like he was people motivated like her, but he was just enticed in a different way. It was strange how people had the same motivation in different ways.

She sat back in her chair and waited for him, her foot tapping a bit impatiently. These days, it wasn't too bad having Koda pop in briefly. His voice wasn't as grating as the others'. However, that didn't mean she was warming up to him. She just liked being around someone that wasn't going to harm her, and it saddened her how volatile her world had become.

CHAPTER THIRTEEN

"**W**hat's that?"

"Ibuprofen."

Blair narrowed her eyes suspiciously at the round pill in Koda's hand. It wasn't the only thing that he brought. He brought a full first aid kit with him and a cup of water, like he was a medic or something. She didn't think he properly understood what tormenting someone that was held captive looked like, but she was glad for his ignorance. She would rather this treatment than what she received before, which left her all bruised, sore, and bloodied.

"I didn't do anything to the breakfast sandwich." Koda pointed out, lifting his eyebrows a bit as he smiled a hint.

Blair felt the corner of her mouth threaten to turn up in a faint smile, but she fought it. She didn't want to seem all friendly with him. She merely motioned for him to give her the pill, slightly parting her lips so he could place the pill on her tongue. She felt her face heat up a bit at the motion, which seemed so indirectly intimate. She accepted a sip of water to wash the pill down, immediately dropping her eyes down to her knees. The heat in her cheeks refused to lighten up as she thought about the action over and over.

She couldn't really help it. She hadn't ever been intimate with a guy before. She had crushes and went on dates very sporadically, but the physical contact was very low and innocent. Even if Koda's touch was technically innocent, it didn't feel that way. It felt sensual in a sense.

"I'm going to clean up your wounds a little. Don't want them to get infected," Koda told her as he popped open the first aid kit. He grabbed a cotton pad and doused it in peroxide before approaching her. He dabbed at the cut on her cheek, making her wince as it stung. He apologized before lightly blowing on the cut, the action so gentle that it caught Blair off guard.

Blair kept still, feeling the light gush caress her cheek and calm the sting. His gentleness made her tense, and it was mostly because she wasn't used to being treated like that. She felt a small dose of warmth fill her chest as he dabbed some ointment on her cut and tended to her. It was an odd feeling, but she couldn't help but like it just a hint. She tried to separate him from the act, wanting to like the act but not him. She wasn't used to someone taking care of her.

"I want you to know that I don't like what they're doing to you. I don't think it's right. I don't think any of it is right," Koda commented as he tucked the supplies back into the first aid kit. His eyes moved to hers, resting there as she pondered on his words.

The problem was that Koda really seemed genuine. That struck her and made it hard for her to turn a cold shoulder to him. He was a big guy, but he came off as soft around her, which made her feel strange in a way. It made her feel a tinge of warmth inside, but she chalked it up to being stuck in her blazer still.

"I don't get why Miles and Ryan are so awful," Blair muttered, wondering why they were so aggressive toward her.

"They're jerks, honestly. They've done this over and over. The more they shake someone up, the more they get paid. This is my first time being involved, and I'm just the information guy." Koda sighed, shaking his head out of disappointment as he sat on the floor in front of her.

Blair narrowed her eyes a little in confusion as she looked down at him. She had no idea why he randomly did that, and her confused look prompted a sheepish smile on his face.

"I'm sure you're tired of people standing over you all of the time," Koda explained as he propped one leg up and stretched out the other, getting as comfortable as he could on the hard floor.

Blair didn't understand how someone so nice could act so misled. He had a heart, but it was like he wasn't brave enough to use it to its max. He was the type that cared, but he still stood in the way of progress because he was too scared to move with the charge. She was petrified of a lot, but she was more scared of continuing to live in the world that she did. Nothing but trouble had come out of that. It was worth being scared to help herself and others. She was used to the feeling anyway.

"How long have you been working for the government?" Blair asked him, wondering how long he had been submerged in all of this. The longer he'd been around, the more time they had to brainwash him.

"About five years. You've been around for three, yeah?" Koda asked, flipping the question back to her.

Five years was long enough for a good amount of brainwashing. They probably scared him into thinking that changing the way things were currently was more dangerous than how people were already struggling through life. It was an impressive feat, and it showed Blair that it all needed to be torn down as quickly as possible. She understood bad people being easily recruited, but it was concerning that good people were also being tricked.

"Yeah, but I guess you already know everything about me," Blair commented, wondering what else was in her file.

"I only looked at what they told me to. I didn't snoop. Just didn't feel right," Koda murmured, rubbing at the back of his neck as he gazed up at her.

Blair was grateful for that. She would feel strange talking to someone who knew everything about her, while she knew nothing about him. It would feel uneven, like nothing she would say would have any originality or element of surprise to him.

"Thanks. I guess they didn't put all of this mess into your job description?" Blair smirked a tiny bit, having done so many things that hadn't been explained to her on her first day. It was like she was doing a completely different job than what she had applied to.

"Kidnapping? Definitely not. I'm honestly not qualified," Koda huffed with a shake of his head, a soft laugh bubbling from him.

Blair cracked a tiny smile, knowing that neither of them expected this. It was a mess that they were caught in.

"You're not a very good kidnapper," Blair admitted, noting the difference in his behavior from Miles and Ryan, who were awful and fit the bill well. Koda was built and could be scary looking if he tried, but his personality and attitude were not on point at all. He was too caring, too in tune to the feelings of others.

"I guess that's a good thing, yeah?" Koda murmured, smiling softly at her.

"Yeah, it is," Blair replied, finding herself matching the smile. She hadn't smiled this much in a while or had a decent conversation like this. She supposed that he was easy to talk to now since they'd gotten past the awkwardness and hateful tension parts. All that was left was to be casual.

"Is there anything that I can do for you before I go? I have to head home soon," Koda told her, a hint of sadness tainting his smile as he stood and stretched a bit, lifting his arms above his head.

Blair's eyes caught the tease of skin that was shown as his shirt rode up a little bit above the waist of his joggers. She felt her face heat up a bit as she glanced away with a shrug, trying to shift her mind away from the peek of abs that she'd seen. Besides letting her out, she couldn't really think of anything. Well, maybe there was one thing that could make sitting here for so long easier.

"Could you take off my heels? They're killing me," Blair asked him, her voice bordering on shy and hesitant. That meant him touching her again, but her feet were so sore from the rigid shoes. She wasn't all that enthusiastic about putting her bare feet on the concrete, but it would feel better than this.

"Of course," Koda replied immediately, almost seeming happy that she accepted his offer. He knelt in front of her, one hand resting on the back of her leg and the other gripping her heel to wedge it off of her foot.

Blair noticed how strong his hands felt on her, how he held her in a way that was gentle and firm at the same time. She sighed in relief as the other shoe slipped off of her foot, already feeling much better. She watched Koda set them on the floor next to her chair before he stood up, a small smile seeming to taint his lips. She wanted to say something as silence filled the room, but she didn't know what. To her dismay, the silence was broken by the door busting open suddenly, Ryan and Miles storming in with a look that told her that they were bringing trouble.

CHAPTER FOURTEEN

"The party is all here." Ryan smirked as he gazed at Koda and Blair as he approached them. He carried a file folder in his hand, which he immediately flipped open as he stopped in front of Blair, Miles coming up to his side.

"What are you doing? What is that?" Koda sighed, tilting his head back out of what seemed like annoyance, like he knew that Ryan and Miles were playing a game that didn't need to be played in the first place. They were just trying to get a rise out of Blair so they could drive her right back down into the ground.

"Pulled some audio from a little place called Orchid Delight. This little birdy told Mrs. Bhatt that the government is always watching among other things," Ryan read from a paper, looking up to give Blair a judging look.

"It was literally a joke. Everyone knows that. It's not like it's a secret," Blair snapped at Ryan, rolling her eyes at how ridiculous his claims were. Yes, she said that, but so did everyone else in this country. That much was known, and all they were doing was finding every little incriminating thing to use against her. It made her even angrier that they were coming near a place and a family that meant a lot to her. The Bhatt family needed to be left alone at all costs. They hadn't done a single thing wrong.

"Seems suspicious, like you were hinting at something," Miles commented, narrowing his eyes a degree.

"Don't you think you guys are reaching a little bit? This is nothing," Koda told them, motioning to the file, which looked like it only had one piece of paper in it.

"Just because it looks like nothing doesn't mean that is the case. She's telling people at a restaurant stuff like this. Imagine what she's telling people that she's close to." Ryan tried to point out, reaching far and wide at this point.

Blair couldn't help but groan aloud, feeling like she'd been through all of this before. It was a constant back and forth between if she did something or if she didn't. They wanted to keep her here as long as possible so that they had a toy to mess around with. They were probably also being paid for as long as she was stuck here, and she couldn't believe that she was being used for profit like this.

"I have no one to tell any secrets to! My parents are dead. I have no friends. I'm not married. I have no children. I have no one," Blair blurted out in what felt like one single breath. She drew the next one in shakily, her eyes stinging a hint. She didn't like saying those things out loud or thinking about them. It just reminded her of how alone she felt in this world. However, she knew some of that was her own fault. She could go out more and socialize more. She could look on the brighter side of things. She knew that she was a pessimist. She was flawed, but she didn't have to be okay with that. The people didn't have to be okay with their government being flawed.

"Sheesh, we're not your therapists," Miles muttered.

Koda clenched his jaw, puffing out an irritated breath of his nose as he turned to the two men. "You've made your point. Let's go," Koda told them firmly, seeming incredibly agitated.

Ryan lifted his hands innocently before turning to head out of the room with Miles following close behind. Fighting with Koda wasn't something that seemed particularly fun to do. It was easier to just leave.

Once they left, Koda turned to Blair, a sympathetic look crossing his face as he sighed. "I'm sorry."

Blair shrugged, tightening her jaw to come off as tough as she possibly could. It was hard to, but she was determined to not break apart in front of him.

"Nothing to be sorry for. It's just how it is," Blair muttered, not meeting his eyes. She didn't like people looking at her like that, as if she was just helpless. She already knew that her circumstances were less than desirable.

"You deserve better. I think you do," Koda replied, his words sounding as honest as they could be.

"We all do," Blair murmured, knowing that it wasn't only her that faced circumstances like her own. So many struggled from day to day, and it wasn't their fault in many instances. They were screwed over by a system that cared more about what was in their bank account than them as people. They could only do so much to change the course of their path when everything played against them. It took her forever to get to a stable place where she wasn't struggling for every little thing in her life. What was scary was that it could all be taken away in a second. She would never stand a chance.

"We have to make the most of what we have." Koda pointed out.

"Some people have nothing," Blair replied, remembering times when she was nearly homeless, when she had nothing to eat for the day. She'd gone through so many sacrifices, and she could look down the street and see somebody going through the same thing as they begged on the street.

Koda nodded, understanding where she was coming from. The side of his mouth quirked up in a small smile as he glanced up at her. "I'll see you tomorrow," he told her before gathering his things and heading for the exit, leaving Blair alone with a hint of a smile on her lips.

Koda was something. He was different from the rest, and she wished that they were on the same level for more things. Together, they could change things. They could help people like they wanted to. It just seemed to be in their nature, and it pained her that there was a divide between them. He was nice and caring. He seemed like a good guy, but she knew he was an enemy in a way. He was playing by the government's rules, and the government was the ultimate enemy in the grand scheme of things.

Blair wondered if she could convince him to work with her. He had the right heart for it. He cared for people that were in trouble. He'd shown that toward her when she was helpless and tied up. Why wouldn't he want to help people who were wronged by the people in charge? She'd just had to convince him that a big change was better than no change at all. It would take a fair amount of convincing because he seemed set in his thinking, but she believed that his mindset could be changed. He just needed a reason to switch sides, to see things from her point of view. She wasn't sure how to do that yet, but she had plenty of time to sit there and think of a way. All she could do in there was think, and that was a benefit and a curse all at the same time.

CHAPTER FIFTEEN

L oud cursing and banging jolted Blair awake from the depths of sleep, jarring her body from the sudden sound as she looked to the door. She tensed up a little, expecting Miles and Ryan to come crashing through, spouting more nonsense, but Koda stumbled inside instead with a brown bag in his hand.

She narrowed her eyes in confusion, not sure what he was carrying or why he was there. She didn't even know what time it was, but she suspected it was around eleven or so since she could smell food. It didn't smell like breakfast, but it did smell really familiar.

"Um... hello?" Blair spoke up, her eyes trailing Koda as he straightened out and headed her way. She glanced down at the brown bag, wondering what was inside.

"Hey. I... brought you something. Well, I got something for me too." Koda stumbled a bit over his words as he caught his breath, like he'd been rushing down the stairs to get down here. He sat on the floor in front of her like he did yesterday, crossing his legs as he sifted through the bag to pull out two plastic to-go bowls.

"So I went to Orchid Delight and got something called butter chicken. I hope you like that. I wasn't sure," Koda explained as he popped off the lids of the bowls and looked around for utensils in the bag.

Blair couldn't even say anything, overcome with shock at the fact that Koda remembered her talking about Orchid Delight and then went out of his way to get her food from there. He really was a bad kidnapper.

"It's... my favorite. Thank you." Blair eventually found her voice, which came out softly. There was a lot to say, but she couldn't organize her words into coherent sentences just yet. She couldn't believe how nice he was being.

Koda smiled before standing and moving closer to her. He seemed to hesitate as he breathed in deep, shifting his eyes to hers. "I'm going to undo one hand, but don't mention it to the others. They'll have both of our heads," Koda murmured as he reached forward to start undoing the ropes that held her right wrist to the armrest of the chair. He let the ropes drop to the floor before turning to grab one of the bowls and placing it carefully in her lap. He situated one of the plastic forks in her hand before stepping away and sitting back down in front of his own bowl.

"This is really nice of you. Why are you doing this?" Blair had to ask, gazing down at the cubed chicken submerged in a creamy, orange sauce. Her stomach growled painfully, wanting to eat the food that was placed in her lap immediately, but she wanted to know why he'd even done this for her. He didn't have to go out of his way for her, but he did anyway. There *had* to be some sort of reason.

Koda shrugged as he placed his bowl in his lap, stabbing his fork into one of the pieces of chicken. "I wanted to try this place, and I knew you liked it. I figured you could use a little pick-me-up," Koda replied before taking a bite of the butter chicken, chewing for a few moments before his eyebrows lifted, a pleased look filling his face.

He just did it to be nice. That was possible? People did that? Blair was a bit blown away, a flare of heat building in her chest. She smiled a little to herself as she ate quietly and slowly, reveling in every savory bite. She felt like she was in paradise just eating this. She just wished she was at the restaurant eating it instead of being tied to a chair in a concrete room. However, she would take any positives that she could get at this point. They all seemed to be linked to Koda.

"That's really good. How'd you come across this?" Koda asked her with an intrigued look.

Blair thought back to the first time she ate at Orchid Delight, which wasn't during a really great part of her life, but it was definitely a highlight. The place made her feel warm and welcome, and that meant a lot to her growing up as a troubled teenager. Food never hurt her.

"I went with one of my foster families, and once I got older and got a job with decent money, I started going all of the time. It's just a nice atmosphere, and the family has always been really nice to me," Blair explained to him, thinking back to the Bhatt family. It was a mother, father, and daughter. They were all incredibly close, working together and living together. They all got along so well, laughing together in the kitchen and helping each other out on the floor. At times, Blair felt a sense of jealousy, wishing that she could be involved in such a relationship. She used to have that with her own parents, but things changed. She lost that and would never gain that back.

"Foster family? Did your parents pass away?" Koda asked, his voice coming out gentle and sensitive.

Blair nodded, swirling her fork around in the rice beneath the sauce. She hadn't really directly talked about her parents or what happened to them in a while, mostly just keeping it bottled up to herself. It was just hard to talk about most of the time, like reopening a fresh wound, despite it happening years ago.

"When I was younger. My father was in the military and got shipped off to some country I can't pronounce. He was killed. My mother worked at a factory, and some sort of virus was going around. They refused to close and forced her to show up. She ended up getting sick and never recovered. Their deaths weren't fair. It's all about greed, money, and power." Blair sighed softly, nearly losing her appetite. However, she was far too starved to lose her appetite due to emotions. She knew she needed to eat because she'd been feeling incredibly weak lately.

"I'm really sorry to hear that. They shouldn't have been in those situations. Mine passed away too when I was sixteen. Their car got torched at a riot. They weren't even involved. I'm sure it wasn't intentional, but... they were still caught in the crossfire," Koda told her, swirling his fork around in his bowl.

Silence fell between them for a few moments as they processed each other's stories, which were both heavy and dark. They both experienced loss and pain. They were connected in that sense, and it affected them through their lives. There was no changing the past. They just had to cope and adapt.

"I miss them. Like the little things, you know? Baking cookies, watching movies together, and going shopping. I never appreciated those moments enough," Blair told him, looking up at him with a sad smile. She treasured the memories that she did have with them, but she wished she'd been able to make more with them. She felt like she hadn't had enough time with them, like she was owed at least fifty more years.

"Painting pumpkins at Halloween, hanging up ornaments on the Christmas tree. I would kill for one more Christmas morning with them," Koda added with a wistful smile, a soft sigh breaking from him as they shared an understanding look.

"Growing up... I thought parents could never die. I just didn't think it was possible. When they did, I never felt so lost in my life," Blair murmured, having never fully recovered from that lost feeling. There was a hole in her heart that was meant only for her family, and it was empty besides some memories.

"I felt like I was just drifting through life for a while. They always guided me. Being in group homes and stuff like that is like being stuck in purgatory. Some people are nice, but it's nothing like being with your own family," Koda replied before taking a few bites of his food, seeming to chew thoughtfully.

Blair nodded, knowing exactly where he was coming from. She noticed that she felt a lot lighter than before, like some of the weight lifted off of her after talking with him. It seemed to help her some, and she was glad that she got some of that off of her chest. It appealed to her even more that Koda understood her. She wasn't alone in her constant grief.

"Do you want a family of your own?" Blair asked him, knowing it was a personal question, but they'd already gotten into the nitty gritty details of each other's lives. They were past tiptoeing around each other at this point.

Koda shrugged, looking completely unsure. He glanced down for a few seconds, weighing his words before speaking.

"I thought I did, but I'm scared of something happening and me leaving them alone like I was. I wouldn't wish that on them. Do you want kids?" Koda flipped the question back to her, an interested look crossing his face.

Blair hadn't thought about his reasoning before. It made sense and only added another reason as to why she didn't need to have kids. She didn't want to subject them to what she'd gone through as a child. They deserved better than what she could provide them with, which meant not having them at all and subjecting them to what they would end up with.

"No. I just don't think I'd be fit enough. I feel too messed up." Blair laughed weakly at the last part, trailing her eyes down as her shoulders slumped.

Koda frowned before pushing his food aside and moving to sit right in front of her. He reached out to gently touch the underside of her chin, tilting it up a little so that she looked into his eyes.

"You're not messed up. You've gone through so much that you didn't deserve," Koda told her softly, a sad look gracing his face. He tilted his head a little, his eyes seeming like deep pools that invited her to sink into. He was strikingly alluring and notably handsome, especially when he was so close to her.

Blair felt like she lost her breath at his touch. Her heart hammered against her chest, threatening to break right out if she didn't calm herself. It was hard to behave around someone that looked and acted like him. In another circumstance, he was a dream. He was so naturally caring and attentive, contrasting from so many people that she'd come into contact with. It wowed her that someone could be so kind, and she took care to revel in the moment. She didn't know the next time someone would treat her like this.

"So have you," Blair murmured, knowing the toll death had on a child. It was awful and traumatizing.

"We'll suffer through together." Koda chuckled, his fingertips feeling so gentle against her skin.

Blair found herself reaching over to place her hand over his, a warm smile gracing her face. He felt like a beacon of light through all of the darkness that surrounded and filled her, and she didn't want to lose that. It could be her guiding light out. She needed to focus on her end goal, of getting out and spilling everything, but it was hard to center in when his smile was so bright.

"Together," she echoed, breathing out quietly. She liked the sound of that, of not being all alone anymore. It affected her more than she realized, weighed on her. It felt like she could share some of the weight with him, like he didn't mind shouldering some of it. It was more than anyone else had done for her.

CHAPTER SIXTEEN

For a long time, Blair thought about the future, crafting her possible steps. She had a lot to think about if she ever got out of there. She needed a plan, a way to bring information to the public. A lot of the files that were fairly incriminating were on her work computer. She just had to bring them to the public's eye, which meant that she had to extract and place them somewhere public on the Internet. Maybe she could post it on social media or some forum. Either of those would work because it would be shared over and over again until it reached countless people. The public would spread and share it for her.

Blair hoped that Koda would come around to her way of thinking. As nice as he was, she couldn't let him stand in her way. He would have to understand that this was something she needed to do. She needed to contribute something to the world, and she wanted it to be something good. What was better than the truth? She would release those secrets at any cost, no matter how extreme. At this point, she really didn't have anything to lose.

She settled back in her chair, gazing down at her right wrist, which was tied back up. It'd been nice having it free.

She got to move it around and stretch it, and she wished she could do it for her whole body. She literally felt sore from sitting there for so long. However, she hadn't had to deal with Ryan and Miles too much lately. They were out looking for more evidence against her, while Koda made sure that she was fed and as comfortable as he could make her.

Her eyes shifted up when Koda walked inside, a yawn breaking from him as he rubbed at the back of his head. He wore a black button-down with black slacks, clueing her in that he was coming back from work. He often visited her after work for a quick chat before he went home. It helped her not be as lonely during the day.

"I wish I could quit my job and not be homeless," Koda muttered as he unbuttoned the first few buttons of his button-down so he could breathe and relax more, exposing a few inches of his smooth chest.

Blair's eyes zeroed in on the skin, which looked flawless. She couldn't help but ogle over him at times. He was dashingly handsome, and he was kind. It was a dangerous combination. She looked up at his face to find him smiling slyly, like he caught her staring, which made her blush harshly.

"Yes. Same," Blair blurted out the words, trying to save herself from her slipup. However, she knew tat she messed up because he was laughing a little to himself now. It wasn't fair. He looked so clean and dressed up, and she felt so dirty and gross. She wished she could get cleaned up a little bit or at least take her blazer off.

"What's the matter?" Koda asked her, noting her random look of discomfort.

"I just feel gross," Blair admitted within a mutter, shuddering a little at the feeling. She hated feeling this way, but it wasn't like she would be allowed to shower. She doubted even Koda could pull those strings for her.

"I can try to help with that," Koda offered with a small shrug, a warm smile crossing his plush lips as she tilted her head curiously. He held up a finger before leaving the room briefly to go grab something.

Blair wondered what she was up to now, but she knew that it wouldn't be something bad. He hadn't crossed her like that yet besides the whole kidnapping thing. He didn't seem to be really on board with that idea anyway, though. She glanced up as he came back into the room with a small, black washcloth in his hand. It looked damp, her eyebrows lifting in realization.

"If I could just take my blazer off, that would be great," she added, hoping that maybe he could do that for her.

Koda thought for a moment before shrugging and nodding. "Just tell the others that I cut it off of you," he told her before approaching her. He undid the ropes, holding her right wrist, giving her time to roll it before helping her get her blazer off of that side. Still being careful, he tied her right wrist back up before untying her left one and pulling her blazer off. He folded it up for her and placed it near her heels before tying her left wrist up again.

"Don't trust me?" Blair teased at him with a smirk. It wasn't like she could do much with one hand free. He could take her down in a second, and the thought of that made her face flush hot. His physique was impressive and built well, making her want to run her fingers down his chest if only she could.

"I trust you. I don't trust the others to not randomly walk in here and see you partly free." Koda laughed out, making a fair point. The others could walk in randomly and catch them, which was something that really didn't need to happen. He took the rag, which was damp and warm, and gently ran it along the side of her neck.

Blair nearly shuddered at the touch, fluttering her eyes shut briefly as she tilted her head up, letting him drag the rag along her skin. She felt her heart start to race, especially when his fingertips graced her skin outside of the rag. She opened her eyes to see him leaning close, like he was concentrating on getting to every inch of her skin. She swallowed hard, wondering if he could somehow hear how loud her heart was beating. She wasn't used to someone being so close to her, but she couldn't deny the fact that she kind of liked it. It was like heat seemed to emit from him.

"You okay? You seem tense." Koda laughed softly, his other hand coming up to rest on her upper arm beneath the hem of her short sleeve on her blouse. He held her steady as he trailed the rag up along her jawline.

"Am I?" Blair squeaked out the words, her eyes falling onto his.

He handled her so well, touching her like he knew how to, like it was natural. It was crazy that she was feeling this way, but it was hard to help. He was entrancing in a way. She wondered if she was just going crazy being trapped in here. Anything was possible at this point. Even developing a liking for one of her kidnappers was possible, despite her trying to fight against those developing feelings.

"Am I making you nervous? I could stop," Koda murmured, his voice seeming to drop low a bit as he trailed the rag along to the other side of her jaw, his thumb catching the soft tissue of her bottom lip briefly.

"No, it's fine," Blair replied a little too quickly for her liking. She hadn't meant to sound so desperate, but maybe she was that insistent on his touch. It made her feel warm and tingly in a way that she'd never felt before. It felt good enough for her to want it to continue.

Koda smiled to himself as he nodded and swiped the rag to the back of her neck beneath her hair, drifting his other hand down her arm slowly.

"I wish we were somewhere else," Koda commented.

Blair shared the thought. She didn't know where she wanted them to be, but it would be great if it wasn't stuck in here. She felt like they were limited in a way. She felt goose bumps rise on her skin as his fingertips drifted down to her forearm, her teeth pressing into her bottom lip briefly in a shy bite. He touched her in a way that was confident, but it didn't come off as too bold. He was just

104

doing what he wanted to, and he was reading her body language, which told him to continue.

"Me too," Blair breathed out, trying to quell her racing heart. It had a dizzying effect on her. She almost felt like she couldn't breathe enough air into her lungs, but she had enough to keep her from passing out under his warm and strong hands as they moved over her body. She found herself reveling in his touch, feeling like she was catching up on something that she missed out on for years.

"All done," Koda quipped before removing the rag from the back of her neck. His other hand had just made it to hers, his fingertips drifting across her fingers before he pulled away completely. He took a step back from her, giving her a bold smile before turning around to go put the rag up.

Blair drew in a deep breath, steadying herself as much as she could. Her heartbeat started to echo in her head, throbbing like a headache at how intense that moment had been. There was so much good tension between them, and it felt so close to snapping. She almost wished that it had. She didn't know what would happen if it ever did, but she had a feeling whatever it was would blow her mind.

CHAPTER SEVENTEEN

The tension between Blair and Koda refused to completely subside. It was there in each of their conversations, haunting them like a ghost. It intensified when they found excuses to touch each other, which were ramping up with each visit. Their talks grew longer, interests being discussed and expressed. Everything seemed to fit together, besides their view of making a societal change. It was the only dividing point, but it was the biggest one that Blair could possibly imagine.

They were having an early-Sunday morning meetup, a paper coffee cup sitting in Blair's now-free right hand as Koda sat in another wooden chair right in front of her. They were finally at about the same level now, and he'd been nice enough to bring her coffee. He snuck her treats from time to time, being incredibly caring just because he wanted to. It made Blair swoon each and every time.

"After my parents died, my life became mediocre. Sad. I want something more for my life," Blair murmured as they entered into a deep talk. They had those from time to time, mostly detailing their parents and their feelings of being lost. They shared that, helping the other through the mess and chaos of those emotions.

"What do you want to do?" Koda asked her, tilting his head a little before taking a sip of his latte.

Blair knew that they were divided on this, but she still had to try and convince him that this was the right choice for everybody. Every decision would have bad consequences, but not changing at all would have worse consequences. People were wronged and deceived every second of every day. Whether the government was setting up dangerous schemes or lying about data, they were steadily destroying people's lives, and Blair wanted to put a stop to that.

She felt like this was meant for her to do. She didn't become an EMT, a firefighter, or a soldier. She wasn't in any of those positions to help people. However, she had access to information that people deserved to know. She felt like this was her chance to make her life worth something. Even if this ended it all, at least she would go out having done something great for others.

"I want to help people. I don't want to be like a doctor or anything. I can't do that, but I can inform people of injustice. I want to give them the information that they deserve and need to decide on what to do next. They are owed at least that." Blair sighed softly before tilting her coffee cup to take a deep sip. Plus, situations like the one that she was in needed to stop happening. People didn't need to be kidnapped to be shut up. It was corrupt and crazy, and she couldn't imagine how many people had been in this position before her or how many would be here after her. If things went right, no one else or only a few would be in this situation.

Koda was quiet, but he nodded. It was like he understood where she was coming from, but he disagreed with her method. He didn't offer any other alternative, so he must've been so lost on what to do that he didn't even try to change things on any level. He just let things pass by him, closing his eyes to what was happening all around him.

"You know that it's the right thing to do. Releasing information slowly won't work, because they'll find the person doing it and kill them like they always do. It has to be quick and all at once before they even notice. They can't silence everyone in this country," Blair explained to him, wishing that she could break through to him.

He was just so stubborn and set in his ways, and she despised how he just stood by and let things happen without trying to make a difference. She knew that she stood on the side for a while, but she was trying to change things now. She was trying to make up for the lack of action she'd taken when she first started finding out bad things.

"Things will blow up so fast. No one is going to be ready for that. It'll be chaos," Koda murmured, his forefinger tracing the top of his coffee cup.

"This country is already in chaos," Blair told him before growing quiet. She was trying to be sensitive to his emotions, knowing that his parents had been indirectly killed in a protest gone wrong. Bad things like that did happen, even if they stemmed from originally good things. They couldn't be stopped at times, but they were good at the start, in essence. Not everything that followed would be bad too.

"We should just move to an island and get away from here." Koda sighed with a crooked smile.

Blair smirked a little, having thought that same thing quite a lot throughout the last few years. It would be nice to just up and disappear to a remote island away from all of the bad things, but she didn't think that that life was for her. Besides, she had work to do here. She felt like she had a duty to the people. She couldn't just abandon them. The guilt would haunt her forever.

"I wish. Sun and fun," Blair quipped, missing the sun on her skin. She'd never been to a beach before, and she would love to visit. Maybe she would go to one one day, but she had no idea what her fate would be after all of this was over, if it ever did end. She might not make it out of there, but she tried to stay optimistic. Lately, she'd been trying to work on her pessimism, but that was easier in her mind than in actual practice. She spent so much time looking at things in a negative light that it was hard for her to see things any way else.

"Peace," Koda breathed out with a satisfied look on his face. Silence filled the room for a few seconds as they both slipped into their thoughts, picturing peace and fun. It highly differed from the state of their lives now, but they each hoped to get there one day.

"We could learn how to surf," Blair added, thinking of so many things that she wanted to do. She had so many dreams when she was really young, but they all seemed to evaporate when her parents died. Gradually, they were starting to come back, even if she wasn't ever going to live them out. Koda naturally brought those happy thoughts out of her, like he was a magnet for positivity. It was what she needed, and she held onto it as tightly as possible because she was tired of being negative so much. That was no way to live.

"We could do anything that we wanted to," Koda murmured, his voice low and smooth. His eyes seemed to drift over her slowly before reaching her eyes, his lips quirking up in a bold smile.

Blair found herself smiling back, a light giggle bubbling from her at his expression. He was smooth and so good at making her feel all warm inside. She didn't want to admit it to him, but the other night, she had a bit of a heated dream about him. She was still tied up, but she had way less clothes on. His hands drifted all over her skin, gripping and stroking all over until she was panting and pleading. She'd woken up feeling heated and shaky, having to take a few minutes just to calm down. He was dangerous in the best way, tainting her mind constantly.

"Anything?" Blair asked him, cocking an eyebrow at him in a bold manner. She hadn't really tried to flirt back at him, because she was sure that she would botch that somehow, but sometimes she couldn't help but act a little coquettish. It was like a game, and she liked playing with him. It distracted her from the chaos happening around her, and she could use the distraction every once in a while. It helped her cope with everything.

Koda's teeth grazed his bottom lip in a playful bite. "Anything," he breathed out, his voice deep and grating against her. He leaned forward in his chair just a little, perching his elbows on his knees. Just the slight closure in distance had Blair's heart speeding up in response.

Blair could've shuddered, but she merely smiled at him before sipping on her coffee. Even if she wanted to do something, she wasn't exactly in the best position to do so. If they were anywhere else, she wasn't sure if she would be able to control herself. She hadn't been allured to someone like she was to him before, which spoke to her. He was something special, something good, and she wanted to pursue it. However, her reality was fairly skewered. They seemed to be on different planes, and she wasn't sure if they would ever cross or if they would ever be on the same level where she wanted them to be. She hoped that they reached that point, but the world around them was harsh, and the elements continued to play against them. It was a whole other game, and Blair wasn't sure if they would make it out of this one.

CHAPTER EIGHTEEN

P eace was a foreign concept to Blair, especially once her parents passed away, leaving her to face the world on her own. She faced chaos and trouble at every turn it seemed like, whether it was within her mind or in the environment around her. It seemed to trail her like a shadow, refusing to leave her as she ventured down the rough path of her life. Obstacles and trouble popped out at her at every turn it seemed like, forcing her back a few steps whenever she tried to make any progress. It was a constant back-and-forth that proved to be incredibly tiring after all of these years of trying to improve a life that seemed to start at rock bottom. She could only be pushed around so much before she grew tired of it. Progress came much slower than failure, but progress had more of an impact than failure.

Things between her and Koda moved along steadily well, more good tension building between them as they became closer and closer. It was hard not to get close when they connected on most things. He made things not seem so bad, and he filled her up with hope. That was the most important feeling for her right now, and he provided her with a steady supply. She was grateful for that because

Miles and Ryan continued to try to drain her of it, refusing to let her feel any sort of good feeling. They fed off of her negativity, which she tried to get rid of. She tried to not let them have the satisfaction of bringing her down constantly, but they only became worse and worse lately. Eventually, they reached their peak.

"We have a problem." Koda's voice suddenly boomed from the door, startling her.

Blair narrowed her eyes as Koda stormed into the room and shut the door quickly behind him. She watched him pace for a moment, his hands lifting to sit on the back of his head, helping him breathe a little deeper. He seemed incredibly stressed, and that worried her a lot. He didn't get stressed out a lot, and she'd never seen him act like this before. Something had to be terribly wrong, and she guessed that it wasn't going to be good news for her. She was a bad news magnet, and Koda couldn't always stop bad things from happening to her.

"What is it? Did they fake evidence or something? Are they sending me to jail?" Blair fretted, thinking up so many bad possibilities that she might be about to face. She never underestimated the awfulness of the government, which would come for her at the slightest clue of something being wrong. There were too many whistleblowers to deal with, and there were too many people willing to carry out the punishments. It was a whole web of awful people doing awful things, and she wanted to take them all down if she possibly could.

"They want to kill you," Koda told her, his tone full of distress. He glanced toward the door anxiously, shaking his head in disbelief.

"What? Why?" Blair blurted out, her heart shooting up into her throat at the news. She didn't think that she would be killed over this, but she had sent plenty of information around regarding strange disappearances actually being deaths that were brought on by the government. She would be another one if this played out like they wanted it to. She would be a file sent around by people doing her job. It all came full circle in the most ironic way, but she didn't find it all that funny. She wanted out of the joke and out of the circle. She didn't want to die, having just started to actually live something close to a life, but what exactly could she do? She was still tied up to this chair and locked up in this concrete room. Plus, she could've been in the middle of nowhere. The odds weren't exactly in her favor at this point.

"Evidently, it's easier to kill you than risk you saying anything. They just don't want to take any chances on you when you know so much and have been exposed to so much information," Koda replied as he walked up to her, his eyes full of worry. He seemed as distraught as her, his eyes shifting all over the room due to nerves that she shared.

"I don't want to die," Blair whispered fearfully, her eyes stinging as tears filled them. She hadn't expected this, and she hadn't expected consequences so soon. She wasn't ready in any way, but she had no idea what to do. There was so much that she wanted to do, but they were trying to stop her at all costs. She would never have the opportunity to do something great and worth something, and that saddened her the most.

Koda cupped her face, his thumbs wiping away any loose tears that spilled down her cheeks. "I don't want you to die either. You're good. I know you are," Koda told her, holding her firmly.

"You are too," Blair whispered, knowing that, deep down, he was. He had flaws, but everyone did. She had plenty, and she didn't think that exposing the government would fix those flaws, but it would make her life seem worth something.

"I like you too much to let them do this to you. It's not fair. I won't let them." Koda gritted out before suddenly tearing at the ropes that held her wrists down. He yanked at them until they fell to the ground with him following so that he could untie her ankles, freeing her finally.

Blair could only sit there in shock, not expecting to be set free just like that. He'd actually helped her, refusing to let her get killed. She slowly stood up, her eyes blinking a few times in surprise as she turned to look at him.

"We can flee the country or something. We don't have to stay here," Koda told her, his hands reaching out to take hers as he helped her steady herself.

Blair knew that he wanted to make a direct line to the airport, but she had an errand to run first. She knew that fleeing the country was probably the best idea for her after all of this. Undoubtedly, people would be after her after she finished up, and it wasn't like she could fight them off.

She had to run, and she wouldn't mind having a partner to run away with. Maybe she would actually get to live her life on an island. She hadn't expected it to play out this way, but it was better than sitting here and getting killed.

"Okay, let's do it," Blair agreed, nodding as she gazed up at him. It was like getting to be around him properly for the first time, encouraging a whole wave of emotions to crash through her at one time. She couldn't help herself, prompting her to reach up and place a hand on the back of his neck. She dragged him down to crash her lips against his, feeling the warmth and softness of his mouth against hers. It was a blissful sensation, one that dizzied her as his hands grabbed her waist and pulled her forward.

Koda tilted his head a little, meshing their lips like they were always meant to. He gripped her curves, pulling her flush against his body as they tangled together in the center of the concrete room. Heavy pants passed between them as their lips continuously collided and crashed, following a chaotic rhythm.

Blair drew her hand up through his short hair, gently gripping the curls to draw him closer. She just wanted to sink into his warmth and comfort, but she had things to do. Those things came before her emotions. They had to because she didn't want to be a selfish person. She'd been around so many, who would sacrifice the world before themselves. She didn't want to do that or be that person. She wanted to be herself and be proud of herself for once, but that meant doing something for her to be proud of. Even if this felt amazing, it wasn't pride worthy.

With a soft gasp, Blair broke away from his lips, which were now kiss swollen. She lifted her hand up to brush her fingertips along her bottom lip, a pleased smile crossing her face as she gazed up at Koda.

"Whoa," she breathed out, having never experienced something so intense. It was like they were one, falling into the other. It was hard to pick herself back up, but she grounded herself, knowing that they probably needed to go soon. She had no idea when the executioner was supposed to show up, and she didn't want to come face-to-face with him, because she had no intentions to die before she did what she needed to do. "Are you here alone?" Blair asked Koda, hoping that no one else but him was here.

They needed to make a clean escape because what she had to do next was already going to be hard enough. She didn't need any more roadblocks in her way, and she hoped that Koda wouldn't make himself one.

Koda nodded, parting his lips to reply until a loud noise suddenly sounded from above them.

Blair looked up at the ceiling as dread filled her, knowing what that sound meant. They weren't alone anymore.

CHAPTER NINETEEN

"We need to leave now," Koda told her, taking her hand as he led her to the door at a hurried pace.

Blair held on to his hand tightly, not wanting to lose her grip of him. If anyone could get her out of here, it would be him. She guessed that Ryan and Miles were here, and she had a feeling that they were either here to kill her themselves or to rub it in her face that she was about to be killed. Either way, she wasn't having it. She was getting out of there. It was strange actually being able to get out of there, but she quelled her excitement for now, knowing that she was about to face the most difficult part of escaping.

Quieting her breath, Blair let Koda lead her out of the room and to the dim stairwell. She hadn't seen this part with her own eyes yet, and she was curious as to where exactly this building was located. It hadn't felt like too far of a drive, but she knew that it was a little out of the way from where she'd come from.

Her bare feet padded up the stairs lightly after him, her eyes wide with tension. She hadn't felt so scared in a while, but she pushed herself to keep going, focusing on the end goal. It all had to be about the end goal.

"Up here is the kitchen. It leads to the foyer and the front door to the left," Koda whispered to her as they went up the last flight of stairs. He turned to her quickly, settling his free hand on her cheek. "Be careful. Be fast," he told her, knowing that things were about to get rough. No escape was guaranteed to be easy.

Blair nodded, drawing in a deep breath through her nose and trying to mentally prepare herself for what might happen next. She wasn't sure exactly what to expect, but she knew that it would be chaotic regardless because she could hear the voices of Miles and Ryan through the door.

"Let's go," she told Koda, wanting to get this over with. She didn't want to wait around any longer. She was ready to go.

Koda nodded before gripping her hand tightly and throwing the door open roughly. He charged into a small kitchen area, dragging her along with him.

Ryan and Miles looked up from crowding over an open pizza box, their jaws dropping open in shock as they stared at Koda and Blair. Everyone stayed still for a few moments before moving again. Ryan and Miles darted around the table toward Koda and Blair, who split up.

Blair ran toward the left, intent on getting through the foyer and out of the door to escape. She felt a hand on her wrist, adopting a strong grip and yanking her back to collide against a hard chest. She looked up at Ryan, a glare settling on her face as she thrashed in his grip, trying to break her wrist free.

"You're not going anywhere, princess," Ryan snapped as he tried to drag her back toward the stairwell, his other hand coming over to grab the black strands of her hair roughly.

Blair seethed in pain, squeezing her eyes shut as she stumbled across the floor. She tried to pull away, but his grip on her hair and wrist were too tight for her to break away from. She even tried to kick at him, knocking against his shins and knees, but he still kept upright. Panic started to flush through her as she realized that she was about to be dragged right back where she just escaped from.

Suddenly, Ryan was knocked down, his grip loosening on Blair enough for her to roll away from him across the tile floor.

Blair glanced up to see that Koda had tackled Ryan and was steadily driving his fists against Ryan's jaw in harsh hits. She started to crawl away until Miles came up and jumped on Koda's back, trying to wrestle him off of Ryan, who thrashed wildly on the ground to try to escape and get away from Koda's wailing fists.

Koda grunted in pain as Miles' knee collided against his ribs, making him crumble to the ground. He tried to throw Miles off, but Ryan hit him from below, making him endure hits from both sides.

Without another thought, Blair rushed forward to shove Miles off of Koda, freeing him enough for Koda to deal another punch to Ryan before hopping up to his feet.

Blair felt Koda take her hand again, tugging her toward the foyer. Blair spotted keys on the small table in the kitchen area, prompting her to snatch them up before he led her out of the house. She took a second to glance around, realizing that they were in a regular-looking house on the outskirts of the city. There wasn't much around besides a few other houses, cloaking the place in a more secretive area. It was a great spot, but she was ready to get far away from there.

Koda led Blair out to the sidewalk where a few cars were parked along the side.

Blair hit the unlock button on the key fob, watching a black sedan light up briefly a few feet away. She wanted to drive, prompting her to rush over to the driver's side and jump in. Once Koda slung himself into the passenger's seat and shut the door, she gunned it down the street, knowing where she needed to go. If they were on the outskirts of the city, she needed to go inward.

"I can't believe we made it out," Koda breathed out with a relieved laugh, glancing to the side at her with a bright smile.

"Me either," Blair murmured, smiling back before turning to face the road. She glanced in the rearview mirror, glad to see that no one seemed to be following her. It seemed like they were in the clear, and she could relax just a hint before she took her next step.

"We could head straight to the airport and take the next flight out. Once we're away from here and safe, we can plan which island we go to." Koda chuckled, seeming excited as he shifted in the passenger's seat.

Blair stayed silent, nodding quietly as she just focused on the road. They could definitely do that. They could go to the airport and take a flight somewhere that was on the other side of the country to give them a little more time to plan. Then they could prepare what they could and choose a place outside of the country to flee to. It would be the safest thing for them because she had a feeling that Simon and the other heads in the government would be alerted of her escape. If she was so high risk, they would've kept tabs on her.

However, she couldn't go to the airport yet. She wanted to, knowing that they could probably have a good life on some island together, but she just couldn't take that step just yet. There was something that she had to do first, and it was more important than her permanent vacation. It was also ten times riskier, but it would be worth it. She had to go to the office and get to her computer to extract the files on one of her flash drives in her desk drawer.

It was the weekend, so nobody should be in the office. She could get in and out. She would release the information somewhere, and then she could run off with Koda. She just couldn't reveal her plan to him until he just figured it out himself.

"I never thought that I would live my life on the run, but it's better than being stuck in a place like this." Koda sighed as he gazed out of the window on his side intently, like he was taking an exciting, new ride.

Blair frowned to herself a little, knowing that he wouldn't come to her side of thinking on this situation. He was one of those who thought that the only way to fix his life under the government here was to just leave and go live somewhere else. She didn't think that was a solution. That was running away. It didn't help anyone but himself, and that being thought of as a solution wasn't a good thing. People should want to live here and be treated fairly, but they either had to leave here to live that actually fair life or just endure the corruption by staying silent and obedient to it. She refused to choose either of those options.

"It could definitely be better here," Blair told him, seeming like she agreed. She wanted to avoid conflict as much as she possibly could, but she knew that it would appear eventually. Conflict was a natural part of her day, and she didn't want to do things his way. They would always be different about this, which was unfortunate because she felt incredibly strong about this. It wasn't something that she could just ignore or tiptoe around because it occurred in some way in her daily life. Ignorance didn't work with her.

"I'm just glad that we're doing this together. It sucks being all alone," Koda commented warmly.

Blair nodded, agreeing with the last part. It *did* suck to be all alone, but sometimes it was necessary to go solo on some things. Some moments were only meant for her. Others were just meant for him. They wouldn't share everything, and their plans weren't shared. They would never agree with each other, coaxing her to remain silent. That was the best approach right now. She wanted to keep her head down as much as she possibly could about this until she was forced to look up and face the noise.

"We're doing the right thing," Blair murmured, talking about one thing and knowing that he was thinking of another as he nodded in agreement.

It saddened her that it had to be this way, but what else could she do? Even if he was distracting and alluring, he couldn't fully capture her spirit and pull her away from her goals. That wasn't in his power, and she refused to give him it. She was driving. She was in control of the situation as much as life would let her be, which was usually not a lot. However, she would fight hard for control of this one.

"There's the exit for the airport," Koda told her with an excited tone in his voice. He pointed to an exit coming up in the right lane. He sat on the edge of his seat, his eyes seeming to widen with anticipation as his eyes trailed the exit sign that steadily approached them as Blair tore down the road toward their planned destination.

Blair nodded in a quiet response to his words, eyeing the exit sign that he was pointing to briefly before zooming right past it, her foot not leaving the gas. She swallowed hard, feeling Koda's confused gaze rest on her. She couldn't find the ability to speak for a few minutes, her eyes drifting to his in a brief moment.

The tension between them seemed to double, threatening to suffocate her in that small car. However, she kept her cool, knowing that the last thing she needed to do right now was to panic over this.

"You missed the exit," Koda told her, narrowing his eyes a little as he briefly turned to look behind him. He turned back to her, looking even more suspicious than before at her lack of response for a few moments.

"I know," Blair merely replied, not having anything else to say about that. She did that on purpose, and now, Koda finally knew that too, shock exploding across his face.

Koda wasn't dumb, so the initial shock soon faded. It quickly faded from a look of realization to one of annoyance and betrayal.

Blair tensed up, bracing for the storm ahead. It was going to be a rough ride, but she refused to stop the car, knowing that the most important thing for her to do was to keeping going and going no matter what.

CHAPTER TWENTY

"Where are we going?" Koda asked her, the words sounding more like a command than a question. The softness of his face seemed to completely disappear as he narrowed his eyes at her, his body tensing.

Blair swallowed hard as she turned onto a street that was a few blocks away from her office. She was so close to getting there, and she got more and more nervous the closer she got. However, she knew that she needed to do this. It was vital and important. She couldn't let her fear stand in the way of achieving great things. It'd done that to her enough already.

"I just have to do this real quick," Blair whispered the words, a deep pit seeming to open up in the bottom of her stomach. She didn't want to betray anyone, especially Koda, but she couldn't let her feelings for him get in the way of her goal. That was selfish, and that person wasn't her. She was going to do this whether he was with her or not.

"Do what? Go to the office? Are you crazy?" Koda asked, a bewildered look crossing his face as he shook his head in disbelief at her. He gazed out of the window briefly, noting the familiar-looking area.

"I'm sorry. I have to do this. I have to help people. Why can't you understand that? We can still go away together." Blair tried to reason with him, trying to calm him so that he didn't do anything crazy. She didn't want to go against him, because she wanted them to be a team. They could do great things together, but he had to stand beside her instead of in front of her.

Regardless of where he placed himself in proportion to her, she was going forward. Nothing was going to stop her at this point. After weeks of being held hostage, she was going to take down the reason why she was in that situation in the first place. It was justice for her. It was justice for the world.

"This place is going to implode. Why can't you get that through your head? You won't be saving anybody!" Koda argued with her, seeming to snap. He'd never raised his voice at her like this before, had never seemed hostile toward her. However, things changed. The divide between them seemed to gape open, and Blair was unsure if she would ever be able to bridge it.

"You're just scared, and I'm scared too, okay? But this can't keep happening to people. The government needs to be held accountable for its actions," Blair explained to him as she turned onto another street, getting even closer to the office. She knew that he was angry and confused, but she just needed him to sit tight and let her do this. Then they could go with his plan. This was basically his plan with an extra step.

"Are you serious? How crazy are you?" Koda groaned out, stress and anger clashing within him as he grabbed the sides of his head and shook it.

Blair flinched at his words, but she kept her foot steady on the gas. She couldn't let his words discourage her. They came from a place of raw emotion, not logic. He wasn't thinking straight, and maybe her thoughts seemed a little crazy, but they came from a good place. She saw what the government did behind the curtain. He hadn't seen all of the things that she had. He didn't understand how vital it was for people to know.

"I'm sorry. Please. I promise it's going to be okay," Blair told him, trying to calm him as much as possible. It was hard to concentrate on her next step when he was yelling and going against her. Everything felt like it was crumbling around her, but she had to keep moving. If she hesitated or stopped, she would get crushed under the pressure of it all.

"Nothing is going to be okay if you do this! Stop the car!" Koda ordered her, his voice seeming to boom throughout the small car.

Blair flinched a little, not liking the loud noise. The car swerved a little, but she directed it back straight just in time to turn onto the road that led past the office. All she had to do was park on the street somewhere and then go, but she had a bad feeling that Koda was going to try to interfere in some way.

"No!" she shot back, shaking her head as she gazed around to look for a spot along the sidewalk.

"I can't let you do this!" Koda snapped at her before reaching out suddenly and grabbing the steering wheel.

Blair gasped, trying to grasp the steering wheel tighter as he turned it, the car screeching down the road in response. Fear thundered through her as the car scraped other cars, tears filling her eyes as she dared a glance at Koda. He looked wild and angry, like a rabid animal. He wasn't going to stop, but she couldn't let him stop her. She just couldn't, and she could feel her heart breaking into countless pieces as they fought over the steering wheel.

"Let go!" Koda yelled at her, trying to swat at her hands.

Blair glanced up through her blurry tears, seeing a tree on the side of the road up ahead of them. Her body shook harshly as her instincts took over, knowing that she could die any second if they kept fighting. He was in her way, and she had to keep going forward. She gripped the top of the steering wheel with both hands and yanked it to the right as she stomped on the gas, sending the car hurtling off of the street and toward the thick oak tree.

The front part of the passenger's side smashed head-on into the trunk of the tree, sending Blair and Koda both hurtling forward. Blair crashed into the steering wheel before being knocked back, the glass of the windshield shattering upon the rough impact. Her head struck the hard glass of her window as she was jostled roughly, sending her tumbling into darkness.

Blair wasn't sure when she came around, whether it was a few seconds or a few minutes later, but she managed to open her eyes slowly. White noise filled her head, crying out loudly as she slowly turned her head, which ached heavily. She could feel something run down the side of her neck, and she immediately figured that it had to be blood. The front of her car was completely totaled and dented against the tree trunk, but the damage was mostly on the passenger's side. She patted the airbag in front of her down, groaning softly at the pain in her torso from her impact with the steering wheel.

Once the noise in her head died down, Blair glanced over to the passenger's side to inspect the damage, completely forgetting that Koda had been next to her until she saw him slumped over the dash, blood dripping off of it steadily. Horror shot through her at the sight, her breathing growing faint as she stared at him for a few seconds. She had actually crashed the car on purpose, not knowing what to do to end their fighting over the steering wheel. She felt she had been about to die, and she couldn't let that happen because she would've died without doing what needed to be done.

Her hand slowly reached out to Koda, who lay still and silently against the bloody dash. His head was turned away from her, and she felt grateful for that. She didn't think that she could stomach seeing his face right now, which used to be so soft and handsome. A few minutes or so ago, it had been angry and hard. She pressed on his shoulder, seeing if he would somehow wake up. She knew that wasn't a likely possibility. He was gone, and she couldn't bring him back. It was too late for him, but it wasn't too late for the world.

Blair drew in a shaky breath, trying to quell her guilt for now. She felt awful and heartbroken, having lost someone she really did care about, but he had stepped in her way. She didn't know what else she could've done, and she couldn't ponder on that now. She had a plan to execute.

With a heavy exhale, she drew her hand away from Koda's still body, nausea churning in the depths of her stomach as she forced her door open. She stumbled out onto the street, ignoring people that were watching. She needed to get moving before the police showed up, making her grateful that her office was just a little bit down the street.

Hurriedly, Blair headed onto the sidewalk and down it, her bare feet growing raw against the harsh terrain. Despite the pain she felt all over her body, she kept going, knowing she couldn't stop. She was so close, so intent on doing this. She literally killed for it, but she couldn't attend to that side of her conscience now. She had to focus on helping people, and the government was killing far more people than her and needed to be stopped as soon as possible.

Once she headed into the building, which was eerily quiet and only lit by the sunlight pouring in through the tall windows, she headed to the elevator, hitting the button for her floor. The elevator seemed to move at a snail's pace, causing sweat to bead on her forehead as she stared at the red, digital number tick up and up until it hit her floor. As soon as the doors slowly slid open enough for her to slip through them, she darted out of the elevator and into the hallway, turning to head toward her office.

Blair couldn't believe that she had actually made it here, but she'd overcome the odds, refusing to let them take her down. There were sacrifices, but those happened all of the time. She couldn't put one above all. It wasn't fair to the others, who deserved to not be lied to or deceived anymore. It wasn't fair that the government got away with all of that without being held accountable for it. The people had to be the ultimate judge, and she was going to give them all of the evidence that they needed to win.

Once she opened the office door and made a beeline to her desk, she signed into her work computer quickly before yanking open the top drawer beneath her desk. She sifted through notepads, pencils, and other office supplies until she found a blank flash drive. She knew that there were so many awful files that she couldn't fit them all on that one flash drive, but she was going to fill its memory to the brim. She turned back to her computer and opened up her files application, finding all of the messages, memos, emails, and documents that she sent from department to department. She'd hit the jackpot for corruption.

Blair selected majority of the files and dragged them over to her flash drive widget, watching a loading screen pop up as it started to import the files onto the flash drive. She drew in a deep breath before stepping back and watching it load, her heart feeling like it was thumping heavily within her own head. All she had to do was release this information to the world. Guilt and sadness struck her when she realized that going to an island with Koda couldn't happen anymore, threatening her eyes to sting. No matter how much she tried to justify her actions in her head, it still made her feel awful. All she wanted to do was help people. She never wanted to hurt or kill someone, and she knew that would haunt her for the rest of her life.

However, if she didn't do this, it would haunt her far worse for far longer. It'd been an awful decision, and it was one that she never expected or wanted to face ever again. She just wanted to be a good person, to somehow make up for what she'd done to Koda, who'd been following his own idea of how to handle the situation. Unfortunately, his idea wasn't to handle the situation at all. He would've let the situation carry on forever, but she refused to stand by and let that happen.

Once the files all fully loaded onto the flash drive, Blair cheered in her head before ejecting the drive, pulling it out of the slot in the computer's tower. She held the drive tightly in her hand before turning to leave her desk. However, someone shutting the office door prompted her eyes to shoot up, a wave of recognition washing over her.

"Quentin?" she breathed out, unsure of how to feel when she saw his familiar face. She felt more panicked than anything, and what made it completely worse was the gun that he pointed right at her.

CHAPTER TWENTY-ONE

Blair felt sadness flood over her, a sense of defeat accompanying the heavy emotion. She'd been so close to ending this all and starting a new change. She thought she was going to make it, but that didn't seem to be the case as she met eyes with Quentin. She held the flash drive tightly in her hand, refusing to let it go as she watched him walk down the aisle toward her slowly.

"I heard you escaped from your kidnappers," Quentin told her, peering over the sight of his pistol toward her.

"How did you know about that?" Blair asked him, narrowing her eyes in confusion. Did everyone in this building know about her being kidnapped? Was he a part of all of this? He *was* a supervisor, so it wouldn't be totally out of left field for him to be somewhat involved in some discreet way.

"We're the information handling department. We know everything." Quentin pointed out to her.

He had a point. If there was any information about her being kidnapped being passed around, it would've run through here. She remained completely tense as he stopped a few feet away from her, narrowing his eyes in curiosity as he gazed at her.

"What are you up to?" Quentin asked her, tilting his head a degree at her.

Blair felt there was no use lying at this point. Everyone thought she was trying to expose government secrets, and they weren't exactly wrong. She might as well own up to it at this point.

"Extracting files to release to the world," Blair replied, tensing up a little as she waited for him to shoot her or something. He was one of the workers most dedicated to the privacy and security of the information that passed through here.

Quentin held her gaze for a few tense moments before lowering the gun with a small smirk. "I was thinking we do social media," Quentin commented, making a confused look cross Blair's face.

"What?" The question burst from her as she narrowed her eyes a degree as he clicked the safety of the gun on and tucked it in the waistband of his pants. She was confused as to what was happening, but she was very grateful that the gun was no longer being pointed at her. That made it very hard for her to properly think about the situation, which still proved to be incredibly confusing.

"We can upload the information to every social media platform. It'll spread so fast that our good, old bosses won't be able to stop it," Quentin replied as he held his hand out to her, his eyes dropping to her fist to motion for her to hand over the flash drive.

Blair didn't move at first, still trying to process what was going on. It sounded like he wanted to help her, but that didn't make sense. She expected him to be against her, but he wasn't acting like an enemy at all.

"I'm confused. You want to send all of this information out?" Blair asked him, not moving from her spot. She had to trust him first, but she wasn't sure of him yet. It just didn't make enough sense to her yet.

Quentin cracked a smile and nodded as he leaned against her desk. "You think you're the only one that hates their job? I hate what we're doing to people. A lot of people in this building hate it," Quentin explained to her as he turned to sit on the edge of her desk, coming off as way more casual than Blair looked.

Blair merely blinked, prodding him to continue explaining things to her.

"There's a group of us. A large group. We want to expose the government for the greedy, little creeps that they are, and we're talking all of the heads and the politicians. We've been at it for a while now, trying to sneak around and download information without getting caught. We've been planning a release party for all of this information, and then they took you," Quentin told her, his smile turning into more of a smirk.

Blair felt heat flush across her face. She had a feeling that she disrupted plans somehow. It wasn't like she asked to be kidnapped.

"That's when we really started to notice that the heads were getting suspicious. Really suspicious. We sped up our release party plans because it was only a matter of time before they cracked the rest of us," Quentin continued, motioning toward where he, Melody, and Dominic sat.

"They thought that I was part of your group," Blair muttered beneath her breath. She hadn't even known that there was a group trying to collect information to release to the public. Her behavior must've just been weird enough to make her show up on the radar of the people up above.

"Right. Then I just got word that you escaped. The reports that came in on you seemed to be pretty insistent that you were going to spill everything, so I came here on a hunch to see if you'd show up. Turns out I was right." Quentin chuckled, seeming to inwardly pat himself on the back at that. "Since you escaping is going to send red flags up everywhere, what better time for our release party?" Quentin finished, beaming with amusement as he held his hand out to her again.

Even if it was crazy, it made sense. She should've figured she wasn't the only one that worked for the government and wanted to bring it all crashing down. She just hadn't expected it to be people in her own department. She wanted to help people, and since that seemed to be their mission, she couldn't see a reason to not go along with him on this. She placed the flash drive in his hand.

"Come on." Quentin invited her over to his computer, speeding his pace up a bit as he logged on to his computer. He took out another flash drive from his back pocket before plugging both flash drives into the computer's tower.

"We're going to take all of these files and send formats of them everywhere. We already started an accessible database linked to them all that we can share," Quentin explained to her, his voice seeming to bounce with excitement as he clicked around on his computer to open up a complicated program that she'd never seen before.

Blair saw various social media icons and code that she couldn't read, but she suspected it was rigged to send all of the information out to where it needed to go in whatever format it needed to be in. It was honestly fascinating and a better plan than she had originally. The government would never be able to stop this once it got sent out.

"Wait, what happens after this? Won't they come after us?" Blair asked him, not knowing what was next for them. They would be wanted, and she had no idea where to go from here. It seemed like some other people would have to run as well.

"Oh, yeah, they'll be after us, but they'll be in shambles soon. For now, we'll go to our base. It's completely off of the grid. Once things calm down, we'll come back out," Quentin explained to her in a casual tone, like he was reeling off his plans for dinner tonight. It was the oddest thing to her, but it seemed like they'd been at this for a long time.

Blair realized she would be living the life of a runaway for who knows how long. She would have to flee to some base and hide until it was safe to come out. Her life would completely turn upside down, but she expected that. She'd known that sacrifices would be involved in this decision, and some of those sacrifices really hurt her. One in particular threatened to rip her in half and drown her in guilt. She ended both her and Koda's life in different ways, but they were both necessary sacrifices. He would've stopped her. He would've kept her from doing what she wanted to do for so long now, and she just couldn't let him do that.

She had to live her life as a ghost now, disappearing from the public and separating from her past self. She wasn't her anymore. She was someone different now, but she liked that. This person did something with her life. This person put others before herself.

"Are they coming for us now?" Blair asked him, already having a good idea of what his answer would be. She had a feeling in the back of her head, like she needed to watch her back. She would probably have to do that for a while, but a life on the edge was better than a life of oppression or having no life at all.

"Probably so. I have a car waiting out back for us. We'll be out of here in no time," Quentin replied with an excited smile as he clicked around a few times. He shifted the mouse down to rest over a button that said *run* before stepping back and turning to her.

"You're the catalyst. You do the honors." Quentin invited her to click on the button.

"It'll send out all of the information?" Blair asked him as she stepped up to his desk, her slightly shaky hand resting on top of the mouse.

"Every file we collected to every social media platform," Quentin replied as he rubbed his hands together in anticipation.

Blair drew in a deep breath and nodded, shifting her eyes to the button on the screen. All it would take to change the future of the country was one click. She couldn't help but think back to Koda as she readied her forefinger on the mouse, preparing to click. Why couldn't he have supported her on this? Why had there been such a divide between them? The potential for them seemed so strong, and she'd finally found someone to care for her. It wasn't fair, but it was a small problem in regard to the problem that she, Quentin, and the others involved were trying to fix with the country.

As much as she wanted to be happy with Koda, their values just didn't align. To her, justice meant more than romance. Passion for the rights of the people meant more than passion for one person. Maybe others wouldn't understand, but she stood by her beliefs. For so long, that was all she had when no one was there by her side, and she was going to finally put them into action for the good of the people around her.

After giving Quentin a firm nod, she clicked on the run button and stepped back to stand at Quentin's side, watching as the fate of the country began its change right in front of her eyes.

J. BRINKLEY

ABOUT THE AUTHOR

J. Brinkley was born in Tifton, Georgia. He writes in the genre of urban fiction and urban romance. In 2019 he was awarded the urban book of the year award by the African Americans On The Move Book Club (AAMBC).

He fell in love with writing as a teen and decided to take up creative writing classes to hone his skills. He published his first book in 2015. He has self-published a dozen novels under his own company, Voma Publications.

His stories center on memorable characters and timeless truths about humanity in all its glory and in all its ugly ruthlessness. His books are an embodiment of his unconventional philosophies about life and love through spellbinding stories that leave the readers wanting more.

Stay alert because he has more amazing new stories for you all to get engulfed in. Learn more about author J. Brinkley at: www.authorjbrinkley.com or on Amazon: http://amazon.com/author/jbrinkley

Join my email list for new book updates and freebies.

http://eepurl.com/g4sW0H

Join my book group:

https://bit.ly/2yt7s1R

authorjbrinkley.com